W9-AAN-964

Just when they thought it was over . . .

Syd nodded to the man running the karaoke machine, and he slipped a DVD into the player. Immediately the bouncy first notes of the eighties hit filled the room.

I chuckled as the music bounced around, nearing the first verse. Syd reached out to one of the women in the front row, holding out her PDA.

"Can you take a picture?" she asked, gesturing to the phone's camera buttons.

Just then a funny beeping sounded, making me wonder if that had always been part of the song.

Syd sighed. "That's a message coming in," she explained to the woman who held her PDA.

The woman handed Syd her PDA back, and Syd sighed, flipping through the screens with a slightly annoyed expression.

Then, suddenly, Syd screamed.

It was a photo. At the bottom of the photo, a message was typed:

Still sure u want 2 go thru with this?

NANCY DREW

#1   Without a Trace
#2   A Race Against Time
#3   False Notes
#4   High Risk
#5   Lights, Camera ...
#6   Action!
#7   The Stolen Relic
#8   The Scarlet Macaw Scandal
#9   Secret of the Spa
#10 Uncivil Acts
#11 Riverboat Ruse
#12 Stop the Clock
#13 Trade Wind Danger
#14 Bad Times, Big Crimes
#15 Framed
#16 Dangerous Plays
#17 En Garde
#18 Pit of Vipers
#19 The Orchid Thief

#20 Getting Burned
#21 Close Encounters
#22 Dressed to Steal
#23 Troubled Waters
#24 Murder on the Set
#25 Trails of Treachery
#26 Fishing for Clues
#27 Intruder
#28 Mardi Gras Masquerade
#29 The Stolen Bones
#30 Pageant Perfect Crime
#31 Perfect cover
#32 Perfect Escape
#33 Secret Identity
#34 Identity Theft
#35 Identity Revealed
#36 Model Crime
#37 Model Menace

Available from Aladdin Paperbacks

CAROLYN KEENE

NANCY DREW

GIRL DETECTIVE®

MODEL MENACE

#37

**Book Two in the
Model Mystery Trilogy**

Aladdin Paperbacks
New York London Toronto Sydney

This book is a work of fiction. Any references to historical events, real people, or real locales are used fictitiously. Other names, characters, places, and incidents are the product of the author's imagination, and any resemblance to actual events or locales or persons, living or dead, is entirely coincidental.

❦ALADDIN PAPERBACKS
An imprint of Simon & Schuster Children's Publishing Division
1230 Avenue of the Americas, New York, NY 10020
Copyright © 2009 by Simon & Schuster, Inc.
All rights reserved, including the right of
reproduction in whole or in part in any form.
NANCY DREW, NANCY DREW: GIRL DETECTIVE, ALADDIN PAPER-
BACKS, and related logo are registered trademarks of Simon & Schuster, Inc.
Manufactured in the United States of America
First Aladdin Paperbacks edition August 2009
10 9 8 7 6 5 4 3 2 1
Library of Congress Control Number 2008932983
ISBN: 978-1-4169-7843-5

Contents

1	*A Wild Knight*	1
2	*Girls Just Wanna Have Fun*	18
3	*Out of Sight, On My Mind*	33
4	*A Brunch of Drama*	38
5	*Seeing Shred*	52
6	*Reality Television?*	68
7	*Heart of Glass*	82
8	*Secret Visits*	96
9	*Past Grievances*	107
10	*Light of My Life*	119
11	*Secret Betrayals*	140
12	*A Dangerous Maid*	146
13	*Unexpected Contact*	161

A WILD KNIGHT

"**A**re we ready to par-tee down?" my friend Bess Marvin asked with an impish grin as she climbed into the backseat of my Prius. Next to me, in the passenger seat, my friend George Fayne groaned. She and Bess might be cousins, but their personalities are *very* different.

"Ready as I'm going to get," I replied, pulling out of Bess's driveway. "Hopefully this party will be a little quieter than the last one we went to."

"You mean, we won't catch any criminals?" George asked, faking a disappointed pout. "I do so love a party that ends with someone being led away in handcuffs."

I smiled. The three of us were headed to a joint bachelor/bachelorette party for George and Bess's cousin, Sydney Marvin. Syd was scheduled to get married in a week, and so far, the preparations for her wedding had been a little *too* exciting. First Syd got a very creepy reply card in the mail. Instead of just information about who would be coming to the wedding and whether he or she would bring a guest, this card was printed to look like the original invitation, and read:

RSVP: I WILL ATTEND.
BUT IF YOU KNOW WHAT'S BEST
FOR YOU, SYDNEY, YOU *WON'T*.

Sydney is a pretty successful model, so if this had been the only strange incident, we might have written it off as a practical joke from an overzealous fan. But then, within hours of arriving in town, her fiancé, Vic, was sent to the hospital after someone tried to poison his drink with jet fuel! Thankfully he'd come out of it fine, but just days later, Syd was the victim of another attack—this time she was given a lei infested with tiny biting ants. That may sound odd—what do leis have to do with wedding preparations?—but truthfully, this whole wedding is a little odd. For one thing, it's being filmed by the producers of *Daredevils,* the reality television competition, as a TV special. And for another, the wedding seems to be under attack. It looks like *somebody* out there really doesn't want to see Syd and Vic say "I do."

"Has Syd mentioned any more creepy e-mails or texts?" I asked my friends as I pulled into the parking lot for Mead, a medieval-themed chain restaurant that would be hosting the party. Over the last few weeks, Syd had received a couple threatening e-mails—all sent from public computers—and at least one scary text message.

Bess shook her head. "Nothing since the shower," she replied. At Syd's bridal shower, we'd gotten at least some answers as to why the wedding seemed to be cursed. Putting two and two together, I'd realized that a friend and fellow model to Syd, Candy Kaine, was the most likely suspect for wedding saboteur. When we'd questioned her, she'd admitted it: she had sent the RSVP card, given Syd the ant-infested lei, and even wrapped up a scary reminder of a stalker Syd had dealt with in the past—a Mr. Silhouette—as a "present" for the blushing bride. Oddly, though, she claimed not to know anything about the e-mails or the jet fuel incident. At first I had assumed she was lying and just didn't want to be charged with any serious crimes, but then, after Candy had been questioned by the police and had her cell phone taken away, another creepy text arrived for Syd:

And we'd known it wasn't over.

"Maybe whoever's trying to destroy the wedding got scared off by what happened to Candy," Bess suggested.

"What?" George asked. "You mean how the police determined she hadn't committed any serious offenses, and how she *graciously* just flew back to New York today because she felt awkward? I don't know if that's going to scare anyone off."

Bess shrugged. "No, I mean that she was caught at all." She glanced at me. "Whoever's doing this must know that Nancy's on the case. You know, that someone's paying attention. That might be enough to convince them to cool it."

I pulled into a parking space as close to the front door as I could get, which wasn't very close at all. It looked like this was going to be a huge party. "Maybe," I allowed. "But if this person is Mr. Silhouette, I don't think attention will be enough to scare him off. That's exactly what stalkers want: attention. And if he can't get the good kind—befriending Syd, or getting her to fall for him—he'll take the bad kind, by just scaring her to death."

George shuddered. "Gosh, this has to be so weird for Syd. It's one of the happiest times of her life, and this totally creepy thing is taking away from that."

I nodded grimly, unclipping my seat belt. "That's why we're going to catch whoever's behind this A-S-A-P."

We got out of the car and started strolling over to the entrance. As we got closer, I saw that the entire restaurant was surrounded by security guards watching every exit and even the big windows! At the front door, where members of the production crew were already clustered, trying to make sure only wedding party members and invitees got in, a group of security guards were further examining all the entrants. I noted that a large metal detector had been installed in front of the entrance, and guards were forcing all partygoers through it, as well as examining the contents of all their bags and pockets. Donald, the geeky production assistant we'd met before, was checking people's names off of a list.

"Jeez," George murmured. "They're really taking this threat seriously!"

Bess nodded. "Yeah, I think that's how they convinced Syd to go ahead with this party at all," she replied. "After all, she and Vic didn't really want bachelor or bachelor-ette parties, but the producers were pushing hard for it. When Syd told them what happened after her shower, they agreed to guard this place like Fort Knox if Syd would just agree to attend the party."

Fishing our invitations out of our pockets and purses, we began the long process of being vetted by production and then again by the security crew. Finally we were able to make our way inside.

"Wow," breathed Bess as we entered the main restaurant—a huge room, complete with jousting ring, that had been decorated in a soft rose-pink, Syd's color. Hundreds of tiny lights twinkled in arrangements hanging from the ceiling, and small votive candles made every table glow. Gorgeous floral arrangements graced each table, and larger ones circled the jousting ring and dining area.

"I guess we should be used to TV-budget-decorating by now," George observed. "But you know, it never gets old."

We walked in among the tables, glancing down to locate our names on the place cards. The three of us were at a table with the three other remaining bridesmaids and their dates. But most of the partygoers who'd arrived so far were wandering the room, enjoying some mouthwatering-looking appetizers, and chatting. Bess, George, and I put our things down and walked over to a group of familiar faces.

Ellie Marvin, Syd's mother and Bess and George's aunt, smiled when she saw us approach. "Well, my favorite bridesmaids have made it." She greeted us with a smile, pulling each of us toward her in turn for a hug and a kiss on the cheek. "How are you girls? Ready to celebrate?"

"We're all doing well," Bess replied. "How's Syd? She's not here yet, is she?"

Ellie's smile seemed to flicker. "She just called—she's on her way from the hotel."

"*Hotel?*" I asked with a frown. Syd had been staying at her parents' house—at least up until the disastrous shower.

Ellie nodded, her mouth tight. "The producers felt it would be best." She glanced around, then leaned in toward us and dropped her tone to a whisper. "Safer. They felt they could keep a better eye on her there. With, you know, all this . . ."

Her voice ran out, and Ellie shook her head as if she were shaking off a terrible thought.

"The person sending these messages," George supplied in a whisper, placing a comforting hand on her aunt's shoulder.

"You know Nancy's on the case, don't you?" Bess asked her aunt, gesturing grandly at yours truly. "It's only a matter of time till we catch this mystery joker. Nancy never lets a crook get away!"

Ellie nodded, smiling at me warmly. "Well, you did find out the truth about Candy," she said. "Not that *she* got what she deserved . . ."

"The police decided she hadn't committed any major offenses, right?" George asked.

"Right." Ellie sighed. "But more than that, Syd told them that she didn't want to press charges. Candy was her friend, she hadn't caused any lasting damage . . ." Ellie waved her hand in the air, shaking her head as though she couldn't make sense of her daughter's decision.

There was some truth to what Sydney decided: Candy's offenses were more annoying than actually harmful. She'd caused headaches for Syd without permanently hurting anyone. Whoever was behind the rest of the attacks, though, was anything but harmless. He or she had tried to poison Vic with jet fuel, and their messages for Syd were creepy and threatening.

"Oh well," Ellie concluded. "That's just one of the many things Syd and I have disagreed on as we've prepared for this wedding. If it was up to me, you know . . ." She gestured dismissively to the decorations and camera crew, which was still setting up. "I wonder if this whole reality TV business has made Syd *less* safe."

Bess looked confused. "I thought you and Syd had both changed your mind about that," she said quietly. "I know in the beginning, neither of you liked the TV idea, but . . ."

"I *do* think it's in Syd's best interest overall," Ellie

replied, but her face remained skeptical. Strangely, it almost looked to me as if she were reading off a cue card. "I didn't like the idea at first, but . . . but . . ." Ellie sighed and shook her head. "Ignore me," she said finally. "I'm just a stressed-out mother of the bride at the end of her rope. But I'm sure the wedding will go beautifully."

With that, she smiled, patted each of us on our shoulders, and walked away.

"Hmm," I murmured, glancing at each of my friends. "There's something strange about Ellie and this whole television business, isn't there?"

George nodded. "I know, officially, she's happy the TV crew is here," she replied. "I just wish you could have heard some of the terrible things she said about TV weddings before she changed her mind."

"And then," Bess added, "she pulled a complete one-eighty. The TV show went from the most despicable thing in the world to this great idea."

I nodded, thinking. "I know what motivated Syd to go along with it," I said. "Money. She and Vic will be able to buy a house and more with what they're making off this wedding. But Ellie . . . I just don't understand why she's suddenly okay with it."

George caught my eye, looking suspicious. "Do you think she's *not* really okay with it?" she asked.

I shrugged. "Someone's trying to stop this wedding,"

I said. "If she still wanted Syd to have a small wedding in a church . . ."

"But Aunt Ellie would never hurt Syd," Bess insisted.

"Whoever's doing this never really did," I pointed out. "They've sent messages to convince her to stop the wedding . . . but the only person they've tried to hurt is Vic, with the jet fuel."

George shook her head. "I still just can't see Aunt Ellie hurting anyone," she said. "I don't think she was crazy about Vic at first, but . . . I just can't picture it."

At that moment a cheer went through the crowd, and the three of us turned to see the happy couple-to-be, Vic and Syd, beaming as they walked into the room.

"Look at her," Bess said with a smile as we watched Syd take in the room, exclaiming over every beautiful decoration. "You'd never know she wanted to cancel this party."

"Maybe she changed her mind," I suggested.

"Or maybe she's just becoming a better actress," George guessed.

Syd looked beautiful in a green silk wrap dress that accented her eyes, her long hair pinned up in a loose bun. As she moved through the room, greeting guests and accepting compliments, she truly seemed to be glowing with happiness.

Until she reached us. As soon as Syd spotted me, her blissed-out expression seemed to melt into one of concern verging on panic. "Nancy," she hissed, taking my hand. "Thank goodness you're here. I'm so worried our little friend is going to strike again!" She glanced around, trying to hide her fear from the other guests, then turned back to me. "Have you learned anything new? Is there anything you can tell me?"

I shook my head regretfully. Despite tons of Internet research and a whole lot of thought, I still had no idea who was threatening her wedding. "But I'll find the person," I promised her. "Just you wait."

Syd squeezed my hand and nodded. Just then Donald Hibbard, the mousy young production assistant, stepped into the middle of the room and raised his hand to get everyone's attention. "Hello?" he asked, his voice barely audible in the huge space. "Can I have everyone's attention?"

It took at least five minutes, but with people in the crowd helping out, finally everyone quieted down enough to hear what Donald was trying to tell us.

"We're going to begin filming the party," he explained. "First we'll all eat dinner, and then we'll enjoy Mead's medieval-themed floor show. After that the men and women will break into two separate groups and enjoy their bachelor and bachelorette parties in the event rooms downstairs."

"Whoopee," George whispered sarcastically.

"I think, in this case, 'bachelorette party' just means, you know—a party," Bess explained. "Syd and Vic wanted this to be the kind of event people could bring their kids to."

Donald was still trying to urge people to their seats, but everyone had started chatting after he announced the plan, and it seemed he had lost control of the room. I felt a little sorry for him as he gestured and yelled and tried to get everyone's attention back with his soft-spoken voice. Finally Hans Eberhart, the very talented but impatient director of the reality show, spoke up. *"Everyone sit down!"* he shouted, his voice loud enough to cut through the chatter. "That is, if you want to get any sleep tonight. And I know *I* do."

Gradually the din grew quieter, and people began to split off and search for their seats among the carefully arranged tables. Hans led Syd and Vic over to their private table right by the jousting floor, whispering some last-minute instructions. Bess, George, and I walked back to the bridesmaids' table, where our fellow bridesmaids Deb, Akinyi, and Pandora had already gathered.

"Isn't this something!" Giggly Deb Camden, one of Syd's old friends from River Heights, greeted us as we walked over to our seats. "All these people! These beautiful decorations! I bet this is going to be a *knight* to remember! Ahahahahahahahaha!"

Snorting, Deb turned to George and firmly poked her shoulder a couple times. "Get it? A *knight* to remember, like the knights of the round table? *Get* it?"

George looked pained. And actually, those pokes looked like they hurt. "Ha . . . ha," George replied weakly, settling into her seat with a stone-faced expression. "Hilarious, Deb. As always."

"Oh! I just love parties!" Deb giggled, settling down next to George.

"Me too," George agreed, shooting a look at Bess and me. "And I have a feeling this is going to be a long one."

I kept an eye on Syd throughout dinner (a huge hunk of meat we had to eat with our hands, per the medieval theme). She was visibly nervous, but she did seem to push her worries to the back burner and have a good time chatting and laughing with Vic. It always made me feel better about this whole wedding insanity to watch the two of them together. However bumpy their ride to the altar might be, they clearly loved each other very much.

As dessert was winding down, Bess poked my arm. "Want to go chat with Syd?" she asked me and George. "It looks like Vic excused himself to the restroom, and she's sitting there all alone."

I moved to get up. "Sure. Why—"

But I was cut off by an announcer's voice.

"WELLLLLCOME TO MEAD, WHERE EVERYONE HAS A KNIGHT IN SHINING ARMOR! If everyone will just return to their seats, we're about to start the jousting show . . ."

Bess, George, and I thunked back into our chairs.

"There goes that idea," George muttered.

As she spoke, the lights dimmed, and bright spotlights illuminated the jousting floor, which seemed to be just a huge pen covered in sawdust in the middle of the room.

"Please welcome our jousters tonight, Malvolio, the black knight, and Romeo, the white!"

As we watched, two knights on horses suddenly rode in from a far entrance, each elaborately costumed in shiny armor and their color of choice. They each circled the ring, waving at the crowd and pumping their arms for applause. The crowd went nuts.

"Let's get started!" the announcer continued. We all watched as the knights faced off in the center of the ring. When the announcer said "go," they began jousting, which was much more complicated than I'd thought. There was lots of dodging on the horses and running around the ring. It seemed that both knights had fans in the audience, and people were very loud about supporting their favorites!

"Come on, Romeo!" Deb Camden cheered next to us. "Rip him off his horse!"

"*Deb*," Akinyi, the maid of honor, cautioned from across the table. "It's just a display, you know? It's all fake." Akinyi shook her head and sighed, looking like she felt very above this whole display. Ever since she'd arrived in River Heights, Akinyi had seemed slightly out of sorts—complaining about her wardrobe, the town, the way she was going to look on camera, you name it. I wasn't sure what to make of it, except that Akinyi must be a very particular person—and not used to leaving New York City very often.

Deb looked a little chastened, and I could tell Bess felt bad. "Rip him off his horse?" she asked Deb, poking her on the shoulder. "Give me a break! Malvolio's got this all wrapped up."

Recognizing a kindred soul in Bess, Deb grinned. "Are you kidding? Malvolio couldn't joust his way out of a paper bag."

Suddenly the cheers and jeers all through the room intensified. I glanced back to the jousting floor, and saw the white knight advance on Malvolio, knocking him off his horse!

"The winner . . ." the announcer cried, "is Romeo, the white knight!"

Deb went crazy, cheering and hooting, and I noticed Akinyi rolling her eyes at her boyfriend, Josh, as she pulled out a compact to check her makeup. Bess booed, and George and I clapped politely.

The black knight mounted his horse again, and they both moved to the center of the ring. I noticed a man with a microphone—he must be the announcer, who we hadn't seen until then—moving into the ring to join them.

"Let's hear it for the black knight!" he called, and the room erupted into cheers and applause. The black knight took off his shiny helmet, revealing a smiling, bearded face. He waved and smiled, gesturing proudly to his horse. The applause intensified.

Beaming, the announcer turned from him to the white knight. "And let's hear it . . . for *Vic Valdez*!"

A confused hush went through the crowd as the white knight directed his horse to the middle of the rung and pulled off his helmet, revealing Vic! I glanced over at Syd, who was beaming and laughing, and realized that, sure enough, Vic had never returned to his place at their table.

"Your white knight in shining armor, Sydney!" the announcer called, gesturing at Vic. Vic was laughing and waving enthusiastically, doing muscleman poses (as best he could atop his horse) and showing off. I looked over and saw Syd cracking up, seemingly totally at ease now—that made me happy.

But suddenly there was a loud noise, and everything seemed to happen at once. Vic's horse, a gorgeous white stallion, spooked and started running for the exit. Vic, caught off guard and still preening, lurched backward—and with a sickening *thud*, he fell off the stallion and landed headfirst on the ground!

GIRLS JUST WANNA HAVE FUN

"Oh my gosh!" Syd shrieked and jumped up from her table, barreling toward the jousting ring. "Vic! No!"

I could feel myself tensing up. Has the wedding saboteur struck again? Whoever it was, this wasn't the first time he or she had targeted Vic.

But just as the crowd was beginning to freak out, Vic began to move. He rubbed his head and slowly moved into a sitting position. Shaking his head like he was dizzy, he sat for a few seconds before carefully pushing himself up to a standing position.

"Vic!" Syd cried again. She'd reached the gate

to the jousting ring, and a waiter ran over to open it and let her get to her fiancé.

"I'm okay!" Vic called. Then the announcer handed Vic his microphone, and he repeated so we all could hear: "I'm okay! Nobody panic! My horse just got a little too excited!"

"Vic, are you sure?" Syd cried, running toward him and throwing her arms around him. "You don't have a concussion? You bumped your head so hard!"

Vic shook his head. "It must have looked worse than it was. Actually, I landed on my elbow, which is crazy sore, yeah."

Looking sympathetic, Syd reached out and stroked his elbow. The announcer took the microphone back from Vic.

"We're so sorry to have frightened you, ladies and gentlemen," he told the crowd. "It sounded like someone dropped a pot in the kitchen, and Vic's horse was feeling a little nervous tonight. But our hero is fine!"

The crowd erupted into cheers, and I glanced at George with a shrug. *Hoo . . . ray?* After all the crazy things that had happened since we started preparing for this wedding, I wasn't sure what to think.

"You think it was really someone dropping a pot in the kitchen?" George whispered.

"Not any pot I'm familiar with, but I guess so," I replied, looking down at Syd and Vic. Any concern that Syd had been feeling seemed to have evaporated. "If not, it seems like kind of a faulty plan. Everyone's fine—except maybe one freaked-out horse."

George nodded as the announcer spoke into the microphone again. "Now we have another surprise for our happy couple."

A murmur went through the crowd as a fully costumed knight—this time wearing a complete suit of armor—slowly walked into the ring. The armor, which must have weighed a ton, clinked and clunked with every step he (or she?) took. Syd and Vic exchanged looks of confusion. A hush went over the crowd as everyone leaned in to hear what was really going on.

"We have a surprise guest for you," the announcer said, turning to Syd and Vic with a huge grin. "Someone you haven't seen in a very long time. This person—a good friend of yours, Vic—is like a modern-day knight: courageous and brave! Does anyone have any guesses?"

Syd smiled, watching Vic as his face went from confusion to total happiness. "It couldn't be . . . could it?" he asked, glancing down at Syd and then taking a step closer to the "knight," who now stood just a few feet away. "It can't . . . there's no way he'd get permission to . . ."

The armor started clinking rhythmically as the

mystery knight started to chuckle. A huge grin spread over Vic's face, and then he started running toward the knight. "Jamal? JAMAL!"

The knight reached up to pull off his heavy helmet, revealing the smiling, laughing face of an attractive, short-haired African-American man about Vic's age. He cracked up as Vic jumped on him, throwing his arms around his suit of armor and laughing hysterically. "*Jamal!* This is my best friend since forever! Oh my gosh, Syd, I can't believe he's here! He's a Marine, serving in Iraq . . . he . . . he . . ."

Vic turned and looked at his fiancée, who was wearing a huge cat-that-ate-the-canary grin. His jaw dropped.

"You *knew?*"

Syd started laughing as Vic looked, amazed, from his best friend to her.

"You *knew* and you kept it quiet all this time?"

Syd nodded, and Vic playfully lunged at her, slowing at the last minute to engulf her in a huge hug. Syd giggled happily, hugging him close.

The announcer grinned, then spoke into the microphone. "Sydney, why don't you explain to everyone who this fine young man is?"

Syd pulled away from Vic, patting his shoulder, and took the mike. "This is Jamal Washburn," she announced, as Jamal struggled to pull off the rest of his suit of armor. Underneath, he was wearing a military dress uniform. He *did* look like a modern-day knight: fit, brave, and full of honor. "He's Vic's best friend since they were both little. He's a Marine, and he's serving his second tour in Iraq. We didn't think he'd get leave to come to our wedding, but . . ."

Free of the heavy armor, Jamal dove toward Vic, and they hugged again. I swore I saw tears dripping down Vic's face.

The announcer took back the microphone. "What a beautiful reunion!" he cried. "Now, you boys will have plenty of time to catch up at the bachelor party. Because it's time for the girls and guys to separate. Ladies, please make your way to the event room downstairs! Gentlemen, you'll be in the party room to the right."

Someone turned on music, which blared Lionel Richie's "Celebrate."

"Old school," Bess murmured. "I like it."

I pushed back from the table and glanced at my best friends. "Shall we?" I asked.

Syd and Vic were still catching up with Jamal on the jousting floor, but the guests moved pretty quickly to get to their respective parties. Bess, George, and I made our way downstairs, where the gentle strains of "Celebrate" were replaced by Pink's "Let's Get this

Party Started," which blared over the stereo system. Downstairs, the walls were upholstered in royal purple and emerald green velvet, and dim, pink lighting illuminated a small karaoke stage. A good portion of the crew and camera men were already set up in the small space, ready to film all of the action. In addition to those cameras, I noticed a video camera aimed at the stage, and Bess squeezed my arm and pointed to huge video screens arranged across the room. "Look, Nance!" she cried excitedly. "We could sing a song and be famous!"

George looked like she'd rather eat paint. "Don't count on it," she warned her cousin.

The room was slowly filling up, and the three of us took cups of fizzy punch from a waiter who danced by in a court jester costume. Other waiters strolled by with trays of meat, cheese, and tiny pastries filled with apples and honey. As we chatted and waited for Syd to come down, Deb Camden stepped onto the karaoke stage and started giggling uncontrollably.

Bess bit her lip. "This oughtta be good."

George sighed. "'Good' must mean something different to you."

"Hee! Oh, hee hee! Okay, I mean, no really... hehehehe!" Deb was turning red, looking from the crowd to the extensive *Daredevils* crew.

"Sing something!" someone shouted impatiently

from the crowd. I didn't see who had yelled it, but it sounded like Akinyi.

"Hehehehe! Okay, okay." Deb took a deep breath and stared at a spot on the floor, seeming to center herself. She paused, miraculously giggle-free, and looked up into the camera. "I would like to serenade you all," she announced, "with a little ditty by Britney Spears, entitled 'Oops I Did it Again.'"

George closed her eyes, looking pained. "Kill me," she begged.

Electronic notes sounded, and Deb began shifting abruptly from hip to hip, side to side. "Yeah yeah yeah yeah yeah," she sang. "Yeah yeah yeah yeah yeah yeah yeah . . ."

George turned to me. "I find myself in need of a distraction," she announced, grabbing another glass of fizzy punch off a tray that went by with a jingling jester. "Who can we talk to?"

I looked around. Standing a few feet away from us, moving in an odd, new-agey way to the music, was Pandora, one of our fellow bridesmaids and Vic's former *Daredevils* teammate—and public romance. I knew Syd wasn't too fond of Pandora—nothing personal, it was just odd for her to have her fiancé's former flame involved in her wedding—and a little part of me wondered whether Pandora might not be quite over Vic. In other words, she would be an *excellent* person to chat up and try to get to know a little better.

I nudged George and gestured to Pandora. She nodded, sending a last pained look in Deb's direction. "Let's do this."

Bess followed as we walked over to Pandora with friendly smiles. "Hey, Pandora," I said casually, taking a sip of my punch. "Are you enjoying the party so far?"

Pandora looked genuinely happy to see us, and she stopped dancing to nod enthusiastically. "Oh, this party is the best!" she enthused. "Everyone seems so happy. Look at Deb up there—her aura is *totally* pink."

"Uh, yeah," Bess nodded, glancing at Deb—who was writhing to the music. "Did you enjoy the jousting?"

Pandora turned serious. "Normally I despise any kind of violence, but since it was all in fun, I guess it was all right." She turned to me, concern clouding her face. "Thank goodness Vic is all right, right?" she asked. "I was so nervous when he fell. Especially when I thought about everything that's happened so far."

I nodded. "Yes, thank goodness it was just an accident."

Pandora nodded, turning back to face the stage

with a thoughtful expression. While she was out-wardly agreeing with me, she seemed to be chewing something over in her mind. Finally she sighed and turned back to face us. "You know what's strange?"

"What?" George asked.

Pandora shook her head. "It'll seem crazy, I know. I know you caught the person behind all the crazy pranks, Nancy, and I know Candy's gone home. But I'm still feeling . . . just . . ." She made a pained face, like it was actually hurting her, whatever she was feeling.

"Nervous?" Bess suggested helpfully.

Pandora relaxed her face and shook her head. "No. If it was just *me* feeling it, it would be nervous. But it's bigger than that. It's like the universe—" She stopped and sighed, frustrated. "The only way I can explain it to you is *bad vibes*. With Candy caught and Syd and Vic feeling so happy, I feel like I should be get-ting *great* vibes about this wedding. But I'm not. I'm sensing fear and anger and sadness . . . and pain, both emotional and physical."

I glanced at my friends, cringing.

Pandora turned to me. "My senses must be way off, right?" she asked. "I keep performing cleansing rituals every morning, thinking it will help. But I'm still getting these bad vibes."

Bess nudged me. I knew what she was thinking:

Should we tell Pandora that there was still at least one culprit out there? That Candy wasn't behind the most dastardly prank, and someone was still trying to frighten Syd with text messages and e-mails?

I looked at Bess and shook my head slightly. *No.* As much as I wanted to assure Pandora she wasn't crazy—that her senses were dead on, actually—I knew I'd better not. We had a better shot of finding the culprit if no one knew we were looking. Otherwise the guilty party might start changing his or her behavior to throw us off track.

"Maybe you're just dehydrated," Bess suggested helpfully, placing her hand on Pandora's shoulder. "Be sure to drink plenty of water, okay?"

But George was moving in for the kill. "Maybe it just feels strange to you," she suggested, "watching someone you used to be so close to get married. Could that be causing your weird vibes?"

Pandora turned to George, and for just a second, an emotion I couldn't identify flashed in her eyes. Was it anger? Disbelief? Fear? Just as soon as it sparked, though, it was gone, and Pandora was back to her usual spacey expression. "Maybe," she replied breezily. "Vic and I were way in love. But past is past, you know?"

Onstage, Deb finished her solo, and two girls stepped up to start singing the Indigo Girls' "Closer to Fine." Pandora broke into a huge grin.

"Oh, I love this song," she announced, beginning to move and sway in her signature new-agey moves. "Will you excuse me?"

And with that she walked over to a man dressed up like a court jester who was juggling pins and began dancing toward him. The jester looked a little confused, but soon began swaying to match her, and eventually started juggling around her. Pandora laughed heartily, and he did too. Even though it seemed they had never met before, they were suddenly in their own little world.

"Kind of ridiculous, isn't she?" a voice asked behind us. We all turned to spot Akinyi, juggling a drink and a plate of hors d'oeuvres.

"Pandora?" Bess asked lightly. "Well, she dances to the beat of her own drummer, that's for sure."

Akinyi narrowed her eyes. "She's a first-class nut job," she replied simply. "Let's face it—the three of you and me are the only normal people in the whole bridal party."

Bess glanced at George and I uncomfortably. "Well, Syd's pretty normal . . ."

Akinyi scowled. "Of *course* Syd is normal!" she replied, raising her voice a little. "Although . . ." she went on, casting her eyes around the room with a less-than-enchanted expression, "the Syd I know would not go for any of this. I'm surprised at her lack of taste."

George frowned. "So you're not enjoying this party?" she asked.

Akinyi sighed and shook her head, the scowl fading from her face. "Oh, ignore me," she encouraged us, reaching out to touch George's arm. "I'm so tired, I don't know what I'm saying anymore. They moved us into this horrible fleabag hotel, and I can barely sleep there."

"What hotel is it?" Bess asked sympathetically.

Akinyi sighed. "The Hotel Bristol?" she said, in the same tone you might say, "the dump" or "the sewage treatment plant."

"That's supposed to be a nice hotel," George piped up, looking confused. "It's right downtown, right? With the circular driveway and the columns?"

Akinyi shrugged. "It doesn't even have a spa," she said with a dismissive shake of her head. "And the hotel restaurant doesn't have sushi. Not only do they not have sushi, but they told me they didn't know *any* place in town that serves sushi after 11 p.m.!"

I nodded, glancing at my friends in befuddlement. "Well, yeah, I think most places in River Heights are closed by then," I agreed, "except the diners."

"Diners," Akinyi said with disgust. "Like I would want to put anything with that much saturated fat into my body! I can't *wait* to get back to New York."

The way this conversation was going, I couldn't wait till she went back, either.

Akinyi seemed to read the annoyance in my eyes because she immediately softened and began waving her hands around. "I mean—I love Syd. Of course I do. And I'm happy to be a part of her wedding. I guess I'm just frustrated by the cameras, the pranks— I just think maybe Syd should have had the small wedding she originally wanted. This huge wedding was a mistake."

This was interesting; I leaned in. "Do you mean—?" I began but before I could get the whole question out, the bride-to-be herself, Syd, grabbed my arm and tried to pull me away, giggling.

"Come sing with me!" she coaxed, clearly having a great time. With her other hand, she grabbed George, and Bess followed with an eager smile.

"You guys know the classics, right?" Syd asked with a grin, pulling us up toward the stage. "I'm talking about Cyndi Lauper—'Girls Just Wanna Have Fun'?"

"I know it," George confirmed, "but I really don't think you want to hear me sing."

"Me either," I agreed, shooting a pleading look at Sydney. "I have it on pretty good authority that my singing can cause permanent hearing damage. Are you sure you want to risk it?"

Syd just laughed, stepping on to the stage and pulling George and me with her. "Oh, save the drama for your mama, you two," she replied, turning and pointing to the screen where song lyrics would appear. "Just follow along and belt it out! I'm the bridezilla, you have to do what I say."

Bess snorted. "Syd," she insisted, "you are *far* from a bridezilla."

Syd nodded to the man running the karaoke machine, and he slipped a DVD into the player. Immediately the bouncy first notes of the eighties hit filled the room. I swallowed and turned to George, who looked panicked.

"Do something," she hissed at me. "Pull the fire alarm, break the machine. I would rather do *anything* but sing karaoke!'

I chuckled as the music bounced around, nearing the first verse. Syd reached out to one of the women in the front row, holding out her PDA.

"Can you take a picture?" she asked, gesturing to the phone's camera buttons. "I want to document my cousin George's first and last karaoke performance!" She turned to George with a big grin, and even though George was rolling her eyes, she couldn't help but smile back.

Just then a funny beeping sounded, making me wonder if that had always been part of the song.

Syd sighed. "That's a message coming in," she explained to the woman who held her PDA. "Let me see; I have to clear it before it'll let me do anything else. Phones!"

The woman handed Syd her PDA back, and Syd sighed, flipping through the screens with a slightly annoyed expression.

Then, suddenly, Syd screamed.

"Aaaauughh!"

She had the karaoke microphone in her hand, which picked up her scream and reverberated it throughout the room.

"What is it?!" Bess demanded, recovering before the rest of us. "Syd, what's going on?"

In response, Syd just held up her PDA so we could see its screen.

It was a photo—of Pandora. Sitting on Vic's lap and stroking his hair. Vic and the other guys in the wedding party were playing poker, which meant this photo must have been snapped just now, at the bachelor party.

At the bottom of the photo, a message was typed:

Still sure u want 2 go thru with this?

OUT OF SIGHT, ON MY MIND

"**O**h my gosh," Syd breathed, shaking her head and looking up at us with a panicked expression. "Oh my gosh."

"Syd, come on," George said gently, placing her hand on her cousin's shoulder. "She's just fooling around. This isn't anything incriminating. He probably didn't even ask her to sit there."

Syd shook her head furiously. "No, no, *no*," she insisted. "They were dating before—you know that! And women don't just accidentally drop into your lap and start playing with your hair. The last time I checked, Vic had a mouth—he could have told her to get lost!"

Gripping her PDA, Syd shoved it back into her pocket and started storming off the stage. "I'm going up there," she announced, stomping through the party room. "Don't try to stop me!"

Warily, I glanced at Bess and George.

"Oh, brother," murmured Bess.

"This isn't going to end well," agreed George.

"Guys," I said, nodding after our departing bride, "let's go after her."

We began to follow, easily passing through the rift in the crowd that Syd had created. Others, too, were slowly following in her footsteps, no doubt eager to see the confrontation between Syd and her sure-to-be-sorry fiancé.

"This *has* to be the wedding saboteur," I whispered to Bess and George. "I saw the number on Syd's phone—it's unlisted, just like all the other messages. Which means somebody at this party just snapped that photo and sent it to Syd to freak her out."

Bess's eyes widened. "So it has to be a guy, right?" she asked. "Who else would be at the bachelor party?"

As she said this, we passed the ladies' room on the second floor, just outside the event room that housed the bachelor party. Ellie Marvin, Syd's mom, emerged just in time to catch sight of her daughter storming by.

"What's going on?" she asked George, Bess, and I, all hot on Syd's heels.

"Um . . ." Bess began, surely confused about how best to relay the situation to the mother of the bride.

"Syd got kind of a disturbing text message," George explained. "It had a photo of Vic and Pandora joking around. I'm sure it was harmless."

Ellie frowned. "Well," she said simply, and began marching to the party room herself. Just then, I noticed Akinyi slipping in the door to the parking lot. She looked at us in surprise.

"What's up?"

George looked puzzled. "What's up with you?" she asked. "Isn't it cold outside? You don't have a coat."

Akinyi shrugged. "I just needed some fresh air."

"Guys," Bess spoke up, shooting a glance at George and me. She nodded toward the event hall. Inside, I could already hear Syd's raised voice.

"Let's go," I insisted, glancing quickly back at Akinyi. With a curious expression, she followed the three of us into Vic's party.

"Why can't you just be straight with me?" Syd was shouting, standing next to Vic at a round table where he and five buddies looked to be playing poker. All around the table, the camera crew that was covering Vic's party had swarmed in, and multiple cameramen were jostling with guests to cover the action from every angle. Syd's face had so much tension in it, she looked like she was about to cry. Vic, on the other hand, looked stunned.

"What are you talking about?" he asked, in the quiet, deferential tones of someone trying to talk down a rabid bear. "Syd, I *am* being straight with you. Pandora and I, that's all in the past."

Blinking back tears, Syd pulled her PDA out of the pocket and pressed a button to show Vic the photo. Cameras moved in to get the shot, so I couldn't quite read his expression as he saw it. When the cameras finally pulled back, Vic looked a little guilty and a little confused. "What's *that*?" he asked.

"It's a text message I just got," Syd replied. "Since you and Pandora are so *yesterday*, why don't you try and explain it to me?"

"Syd," Vic said gently, reaching out to take her hand, which Syd then pulled away. "Syd. This was totally innocent. Pandora was just fooling around for the cameras." He glanced up at a crew member, who silently shook his head. Vic and Syd both knew they weren't supposed to mention the cameras in front of the cameras. It shattered the appearance of "reality."

Sighing, Vic looked around for Pandora, who I now noticed was standing about ten feet behind him. After a few seconds, she seemed to figure out that Vic was waiting for her to defend him, and she echoed breezily, "Yeah, I was just fooling around." She paused and looked directly into one of the cameras aimed at her. "You know how *wild and free* I can be!"

I watched Pandora's expression, feeling uneasy. After a few seconds, I realized why: Pandora didn't look upset at all. If the situation were truly innocent—if she really hadn't done anything wrong—wouldn't she be upset to see Syd falsely accuse her? But instead, Pandora almost looked pleased by the attention she was getting. She shrugged, facing Syd.

Syd looked from Pandora slowly back to Vic. Her jaw was trembling, but she kept her mouth taut, as though she were too angry to give in to tears. She looked at her fiancé and shook her head, an expression of total despair washing over her pretty features.

"All this time, Vic, I've always trusted you," she said quietly, as though she and Vic were alone in their living room. "But maybe whoever sent this text is right. Maybe I *should* have my doubts about you!"

Behind her, Ellie Marvin stepped closer and reached out to touch her daughter's shoulder, but Syd pulled away. The cameras pulled in closer, no doubt hoping to catch a dramatic pronouncement.

"I can't do this anymore!" she went on, her voice rising above the murmurs of the crowd watching and the music still blaring from the stereo. "At least, not like this." She grabbed her left hand and jerked off her ring, flinging it at Vic's head.

"The wedding is off!"

A BRUNCH OF DRAMA

The next morning I picked up Bess and George in my Prius and headed for the Hotel Bristol, where we were meeting Syd—and what remained of the bridal party—for brunch.

"So what do we think *really* happened?" Bess asked as we pulled into the parking lot to the rear of the hotel. "Have you given it any more thought, Nance? Who do we think set Vic up?"

I smiled, pulling into a parking space and shutting off the car. "Who, me?" I asked. "Did I give any more thought to this last night? Hmmm, let me try to remember."

George snorted, leaning forward from the backseat. "A better question would be, did you sleep at all, Nance?" she asked. "And what's the working theory now? I know you've been going over this all night."

"Well," I affirmed, "I *did* talk to Vic before we left last night, but he wasn't in the best place to help me."

"He seemed pretty crushed," Bess agreed, biting her lip.

"Yeah." I sighed. It was hard to watch a couple who so clearly loved each other going through so much strife. "He was really stunned by Syd's announcement. He must have told me a hundred times: Pandora just dropped into his lap, and someone must have snapped the picture in the two seconds or so before he stood up and knocked her off."

George looked at me, her eyes holding a suspicious gleam. "Did you believe him?" she asked. "Because another theory is, he really *was* flirting with Pandora, and whoever snapped the picture was just being a friend to Syd."

I shrugged. "I really believe him," I affirmed. "If he was faking being crushed, then he's a far better actor than I ever would have thought. And I mean, we can't be a hundred percent sure of anything in this case. But I do believe that Vic is really devoted to Syd."

Bess frowned. "This may be a dumb question, but

did Vic notice who shot the photo?" she asked. "Did he have any idea who might have set him up?"

I shook my head. "No. He said he couldn't think of anyone."

"Hmm." Bess sighed, looking thoughtful.

"I do have one theory though," I said, pulling out my own PDA and pressing a few buttons. "It can't be anyone who's in this photo, right?"

Lifting up my cell phone, I showed Bess and George the photo on the screen: the same photo Syd had freaked out over, showing Pandora sitting on Vic's lap at the poker table.

"Whoa! How did you get a copy?" George asked, moving closer to get a better look.

I smiled. "Before we left, I asked to borrow Syd's phone," I replied. "Then I just forwarded the message to myself. I figured she was too upset to bother her with it."

"Huh," Bess murmured, leaning in to get a better look.

The photo was small, and zoomed in close on Pandora and Vic. But still, if I looked carefully and squinted really hard, I could make out most of Vic's friends and groomsmen in the crowd.

"The only guys missing," I said as George and Bess squinted to make out all the people in the photo, "are Jamal and Dragon. Which means our suspects are . . ."

". . . Jamal and Dragon," George piped up with an *of course* tone to her voice.

"But that's not all," Bess put in. "We also saw Aunt Ellie and Akinyi up by the boys' party room. They could have very easily snapped the photo, then run outside or into the ladies' room to send it to Syd."

I nodded. "Or Pandora," I added.

"But she's in the photo!" George cried.

I shrugged. "She is, but she also set the whole thing in motion, dropping into Vic's lap and aggressively flirting with him," I pointed out. "I'm not totally convinced that was just a coincidence. Maybe Pandora set Vic up, and got an accomplice at the party to snap the photo."

George frowned. "And there's a whole other slew of suspects you haven't mentioned yet."

I turned in my seat to face her. "Who?"

George shrugged. "The crew?" she asked. "I mean, I don't know what the motive would be. But that's a lot more suspects right there."

Bess let out a long breath. "Whew. Too many suspects."

George nodded sadly. "And this whole thing may be a moot point," she suggested, "now that the wedding's been cancelled. Maybe now that the wedding is called off, the wedding saboteur will back off, figuring he or she got what he wanted."

I shook my head, frowning. "I don't care if this person *did* get exactly what he or she wanted," I insisted. "Even if Syd and Vic never speak to each other again—and I really hope that doesn't happen—I swear, I'm going to find the person who did this."

Bess and George nodded grimly.

"Well," George said. "I think we can knock Jamal off the suspect list. He's Vic's best friend since forever, and he wasn't even here for the jet fuel incident."

Bess nodded, but I wasn't quite ready to rule anybody out. "He could have an accomplice—"

"Nance," Bess said gently, "come on. You're overthinking this. That's one suspect down."

I nodded slowly. "And I don't really see why anyone in the crew would be involved," I admitted. "They all seem pretty genuine to me. And none of them have a personal connection to Vic or Syd, or any reason to want to see them this miserable."

Bess looked thoughtful. "That makes sense. So let's think about Dragon, Pandora, Ellie, and Akinyi."

"Dragon's the new star of *Daredevils*," George pointed out. "He might be trying to spice things up to increase the ratings—and his own popularity!"

I nodded. "Definitely possible," I agreed. "And Pandora—well, her motive would be obvious. She's not over Vic."

Bess nodded. "And that's looking more and more likely."

"Akinyi?" George asked, looking skeptical.

"Who knows what her problem is?" asked Bess.

"Whatever's going on with her, she's seemed very down on this wedding from the beginning," I said. "She just gets more and more irritable. Maybe she would even sabotage the wedding to end it all so she could go home?"

Bess sighed, shaking her head. "Maybe. *Something's* definitely bothering her."

"What about Aunt Ellie?" George asked, looking perplexed. "Honestly, a big part of me can't even believe we're seriously considering her. She's the sweetest, most cookie-bakingest mom you could imagine. Why would she sabotage Syd's wedding?"

I sighed. "I admit, I'm not one hundred percent sure. But when we spoke last night, she seemed pretty frustrated by the way this televised wedding was going."

Bess furrowed her brows. "But she agreed to it," she pointed out. "Remember, Nance, she and Syd were *both* worried about how this TV thing would play out, but they came around when they realized how much Vic wanted it and how it would help Vic and Syd start a nest egg."

"I know," I agreed, "but maybe Ellie has changed her mind?"

George frowned. "Can you really see Aunt Ellie trying to poison Vic with jet fuel?"

I sighed. George was right: unless Ellie had a secret evil side, it was pretty hard to imagine her hurting anyone. "I don't know," I admitted. "I don't know anything at this point except that Dragon, Jamal, Pandora, Akinyi, and Ellie all had the opportunity to get that photo to Syd."

Bess nodded sympathetically and glanced at her watch. "Maybe we should go in," she suggested.

I opened my door eagerly. "Let's go," I agreed, "and hopefully get some more information!"

We entered the hotel through the back door and rode up in the elevator to the Bristol Restaurant, where we were meeting Syd and her bridesmaids. The Hotel Bristol was a historic hotel that had been operating for almost one hundred years. It was probably the nicest place to stay in River Heights. Cushy oriental rugs carpeted the floors, and black-and-white photos framed in cherrywood lined the walls, showing off the hotel's history. There were photos from the Great Depression, from a blizzard in 1964, from a town celebration in the 1980s . . . the most recent was a photo from the hotel's swanky party on New Year's Eve 2000. Revelers in evening wear raised their champagne glasses high, laughing and shouting.

"There she is," said Bess in a grave tone, and I followed her gaze to an exhausted-looking, bleary-eyed Syd. She sat in the center of a large table off to the side of the restaurant, dabbing at her red-rimmed eyes with a tissue. Her mom, Ellie, sat close by her side, rubbing her shoulder and whispering into her ear. Syd didn't look terribly comforted, though. Tears still leaked from her eyes, and she kept turning away from her mother to sob.

"Poor Syd," George said softly. I nodded, and we watched Akinyi approach Syd from the other side and envelop her in a hug. Ellie patted her daughter's shoulder and slipped away, walking toward us. When she spotted the three of us at the entrance to the restaurant, she smiled sadly.

"Girls," she greeted us, touching Bess's arm. "I'm so glad you could come. Syd needs her friends right now."

"How is she?" I asked. I had a feeling that was a dumb question, since any fool could see how distraught Syd was, but I wanted to hear how Ellie would describe it.

"She's not good," Ellie replied. "She's having a very rough time with all this."

I tried to look as sympathetic as possible. "Do you think she and Vic might still get married?" I asked.

Ellie looked distraught. "Maybe," she said skeptically. "It's just very hard to predict at this point. I think Syd is emotionally exhausted."

"Maybe once this TV special blows over, they could have the intimate wedding I know you wanted," I said gently.

Ellie looked surprised. "*She* wanted," she corrected me. "Syd wanted a small wedding in the beginning too."

I nodded. "But just maybe—this will all work out for the best. Maybe they can have the wedding they originally wanted."

Ellie sighed. "I hope so," she agreed. "Overall, I just want Syd to be happy. And I know she truly loves Vic. I was up all night with her, and she was just crying and crying. She's so confused and exhausted from everything. I think more than anything, she just wants to be with Vic."

I nodded. Those really didn't sound like the words of a mother who wanted to frighten her daughter, or sabotage her wedding. But still—I supposed anything was possible.

As Ellie excused herself to run up to her room to grab some more tissues, Bess, George, and I headed in to say hello to Syd. "You know what's weird?" George asked as we crossed the restaurant.

"What?" I asked.

George gestured all around the restaurant, even back toward the lobby. "No cameras," she pointed out.

She was right. It was kind of amazing, actually, how completely I had begun to associate Syd's wedding with a huge television crew.

"Now that the wedding's off," Bess said, "I guess the cameras are too."

Syd looked up at that moment and spotted us approaching. "Oh!" she cried, her eyes brimming with tears. "Bess, George, and Nancy. I'm so glad you're here!"

We each hugged her, and Bess said, "Oh, Syd, we're so sorry."

"Thanks," Syd said quietly, wiping her eyes.

"Do you think you might get back together?" George asked, direct and to the point as always. "I know you love him, Syd. And I just want to see you happy."

Syd sniffled. "I'm not sure," she whispered. "I'm just so, so tired of all of it right now. I know I love him . . . I just . . . I don't know. It's such a relief not to have the cameras for once."

I leaned forward to pat her shoulder, seeing how confused she was. "I know you'll figure it out, Syd."

She smiled gratefully.

The three of us took our seats, and slowly the rest

of the bridal party filled in. Akinyi ran right over to hug Syd and wipe her eyes. Deb stroked her hair and told her to stay strong. The only member of the bridal party that didn't show was Pandora. Akinyi told us she felt too awkward.

"Believe me," she said, shaking her head dismissively. "That girl has nothing but regrets right now."

When Ellie returned, everyone who'd been invited to the brunch was there. Ellie stroked her daughter's arm and looked at all of us. "Thank you for coming to support Syd," she told us. "Shall we say grace before we eat?"

We all bowed her heads, and just then, I could have sworn I heard violin music coming from the hallway. Was it possible? I glanced at George out of the corner of my eye, and I could tell she heard it too.

"What is that?" I mouthed, and she shrugged in confusion.

As I was starting to doubt our sanity, the music got louder. We all turned our heads as it became clearer that the violinists were moving toward the restaurant entrance. Then, suddenly, there they were, at the doorway—three tuxedoed violinists, followed closely by . . . *Vic*!

He was wearing a freshly-pressed suit and carrying a huge bouquet of red roses. "Sydney," he announced in his deep voice, and Sydney's head jerked up. "I love you and I always will. I'm so sorry that I caused you so much pain. Will you ever forgive me?"

Syd looked stunned, and just as she found her voice to answer, Vic held up his hand to stop her.

"Wait," he announced. "Before you answer, let me sing you a song I wrote. I stayed up all night writing this for you."

He nodded at the violin players, and they began playing. Bess nudged me and I looked up. She just shook her head and mouthed, "Wow."

No kidding!

Vic began singing:

> *Syyyyyyyyydney!*
> *I think of you and I get diiiizzy*
> *You are the love of my life*
> *Without you it's only pain and strife*
> *Oh Sydney, I love you so much I learned to play*
> *   the fife!*

As I glanced at George in amazement, Vic pulled a tiny flute out of his jacket pocket and began blowing into it. Tiny, shrill notes emerged, and George widened her eyes.

"He sounds like a bird on helium!" she hissed at me.

But Vic was done with his fife interlude, and was singing again.

>Marry me, my love
>My little red-haired dove
>I'm like a hand and you're the glove
>Without you I get cold!

George was just shaking her head now, trying not to laugh.

>I want to be with you forever
>Come on it's now or never
>I want you to be my child's mother
>I'll never love another
>Like I love you SYYYYYYYYYDNEEEEEEEY!

The violins blazed into a crushing final crescendo, and Vic threw out his arms, waving them wildly.

When the music stopped, no one seemed to know what to do. Everyone looked at Syd, who was—no, she couldn't be—no, she was—crying.

"Oh, Vic," she whispered.

"Oh, brother," George muttered beside me.

Syd stood up and, after just a moment's hesitation, ran around her table to Vic. She threw her arms around him, and he enfolded her in a huge embrace.

"Sydney!" he said when they parted. "When you called off our wedding last night, my life lost all meaning. What does the future mean to me if I don't get to spend it with you?"

Syd beamed, but then seemed to notice something. She looked over Vic's shoulder, then at the violinists that flanked him, and finally back at us. "Vic," she asked, "where are the cameras?"

Vic's face broke into a smile. "I sent Dragon off to jump into the river and distract them! I wanted this moment to be just between me and you."

Syd blinked back tears, shaking her head. "Oh, Vic," she whispered.

Vic nodded. "Now," he said softly, "will you do it, Syd? Will you take me back? Will you marry me?"

Syd kept blinking, unable to hold back the tears as she looked at her former fiancé. Yes! she cried, and Vic yelped, picking her up and swinging her into the air.

Syd erupted into laughter. I glanced at George— she was wiping her eye!

"What?" she whispered, seeing my amused expression. "That was touching, okay?"

Syd was beaming as Vic put her back down on the ground, and she turned to face all of us. "The wedding's back on!" she announced happily.

SEEING SHRED

Two days later Bess, George, and I found ourselves back at the bridal shop with Akinyi, Deb, Pandora, and Syd, who was having her final dress fitting. Originally Syd was going to go alone, but as she told us, when the producers (who were *beyond* thrilled that the wedding—and thus their TV show—was back on) heard about the trip, they asked Syd to gather all of us so they could film it for the special.

Syd had already been fitted once, but had been interrupted by some bad news about Akinyi and Candy's dresses—something we later found out Candy herself was responsible for. Now we were looking forward to seeing Syd, sure to look gorgeous in her wedding dress.

"It feels good to sit down," Bess observed, sighing contentedly as we sunk into the cushy chintz sofa that took up most of the waiting area.

"Definitely," I agreed. Ever since Syd had announced the wedding was back on, all of us brides-maids had been caught up in wedding-preparation tasks: printing out the programs, making the center-pieces, even cooking up dozens of batches of Vic's favorite meringue cookies to slip into fancy lace bags as wedding favors. Ellie told us the *Daredevils* produc-ers had actually offered to pay for fancy floral center-pieces and professionally printed programs, but Syd had balked at the idea.

"She always wanted her wedding to have that spe-cial, homemade touch," Ellie told us with a smile.

"That's lovely," George, who'd been in charge of assembling programs, had replied. "Or I'm sure I'll find it lovely when all my paper cuts heal."

"When *I* get married," Bess began now, and George groaned. This wasn't the first such pronouncement Bess had made. Over the last few days, we'd already learned that Bess would outfit her bridesmaids in yel-low; that she would have a tower of cupcakes rather than a traditional wedding cake; and that her first dance with her new husband would be to "My Heart

Will Go On" from the movie *Titanic*. "I'm going to do it like Syd did. You two will pitch in, right? Maybe I'll have little jars of jam as my wedding favors. I think I'd like to arrange my own flowers, too."

"When you get married," George said, "I predict I will have pressing business in Japan."

"Me too," I agreed. "Or maybe Timbuktu."

Bess rolled her eyes. "You're just saying that because you're tired," she insisted. "As soon as this wedding's over, you'll miss it."

At that moment Ellie walked out of Syd's dressing room and gestured to Hans, who was settled on a hard bench across the room. Behind us the television cameras and lights were all set up, ready to get the shot. It was kind of amazing how quickly we'd gotten used to being surrounded by a television crew.

"Are you ready?" Ellie asked Hans, who glanced up curiously. "They're just having some trouble finding Syd's dress, but as soon as they locate it, she's going to put it right on."

"We're ready," Hans confirmed, gesturing to the crew behind him. "Everyone's all set up here. Just waiting on you."

Ellie nodded, looking eager to please. We'd all been waiting in the bridal shop for about half an hour already. And while Hans hadn't mentioned it, we all knew at the outset of the shoot that the crew hoped to be back at the hotel by lunchtime to shoot a bas-ketball game between Vic and his groomsmen.

Bess, George, Deb, and I were the only bridesmaids remaining in the waiting area. Akinyi, who'd seemed restless and jumpy ever since we first arrived, had gone outside to talk on her cell phone. And Pandora had wandered off long ago, muttering something about the wedding industrial complex and how she much preferred dresses made from organic silk.

Suddenly we heard footsteps on the stairs lead-ing up from the alterations department, and I could see Hans and the crew start to straighten up. As the steps got closer, we all leaned forward eagerly to see the sales clerk coming up with Syd's dress. But when the young blond girl emerged, she was clearly upset, her face bright pink as she shook her head and ran toward Ellie. In her arms was a pile of fringed silk.

"I'm so, so sorry," the girl apologized, parting her arms to let the silk dress fall between them. "I have no idea how this happened! I'm so sorry!"

Behind me, I was vaguely aware of cameras turn-ing on, lights pointing toward the action. But I was too invested in the scene to pay much attention.

We all looked at the dress in her arms, and I gasped. The dress wasn't supposed to be fringed at all. The delicate, unfinished ends I'd seen weren't intended—

the dress looked like it had been shredded with a pair of scissors!

Ellie took in a quick breath, but she seemed to recover quickly, as though she were now used to these little "surprises." "Sydney," she called in a serious tone, "I think you'd better come look at this."

"What is it, Mom?"

Syd, still dressed in a casual sweater dress, stepped out from the dressing area. She followed her mother's gaze to her dress, and all the color seemed to drain from her face. "Oh my gosh."

The sales girl held the dress up by the shoulders, and we all gasped at the extent of the damage. The beautiful, elegant silk column had been shredded by hundreds of jagged cuts all over the bodice. It hung in tatters, shredded ends unraveling and threads hanging from every inch. It was clear there was no way Syd could wear this dress in just a few days. And sadly, it was also pretty clear that there was no way the alterations department could fix it.

"I'm so sorry," the sales girl said again, "but there's no way we can fix this, and we don't have enough time to order a new dress for you."

Syd's face was frozen in shock. Before she could react, a shrill *beep* sounded from her pocket. Glancing down, she pulled out her PDA and looked at the screen. I cringed, knowing what she would find there.

Shaking her head in disbelief, Syd shrieked and began to cry. "This isn't happening," she sobbed, turning to her mother. "Mom, tell me this isn't happening."

As Ellie comforted her daughter and Deb moved in to pat Syd's back, I stood up and gently took the PDA from Syd's hand. Bess and George crowded in behind me to get a good look.

Just like before, the text came from an unlisted number.

IF U GO THRU WITH THIS, UR DREAMS WILL BE SHREDDED JUST LIKE THIS DRESS.

I heard Bess suck in her breath. "Wow."

"Major wow," George agreed, looking disgusted. "This guy just gets creepier and creepier."

"Or *girl*," I said meaningfully, and I could see my friends considering that. Our suspect list still contained three women: Akinyi, Pandora, and, perhaps less likely, Ellie.

"What does it say, what does it say?" a voice asked behind me as an arm reached out and grabbed the PDA from my hand. "Oooooh!"

I turned around and saw Pandora staring goggle-eyed at the screen.

"When did you come in?" George asked skeptically. "I thought you wandered off."

Pandora stared at the text message for a few seconds before looking up, her usual spacey expression back in place. "I went outside to meditate for a few minutes," she replied quickly, then turned to me. "Nancy! This is just what I was telling you about! Don't you see, the bad vibes were right! There *is* still someone trying to stop this wedding!"

I stared back at Pandora blankly, feeling a little overwhelmed. *So they know now,* I thought. It would only be a matter of minutes before the whole bridal party was buzzing about the wedding saboteur. And once that happened, whoever was behind this would know everyone was looking for her (or him)—and my job would get a lot harder.

"But that's *impossible!*" I heard Syd cry, and I turned back to listen in on their conversation.

"I'm afraid it's true," the sales girl said, shaking her head and sadly stroking the ruined dress. "Our manager said she hung this dress on the door of the alterations room first thing this morning—which is why I couldn't find it. And when she hung it up, it was in pristine condition. That means whoever did this, did it this morning."

"What time is it now?" I asked, frowning.

Ellie glanced at her watch. "It's just ten-thirty," she replied.

Ten-thirty. The shop had opened at ten, and our

entourage had arrived at ten on the dot. That meant that while we all lounged around waiting—and while our poor sales girl had searched the inventory for Syd's dress—someone had snuck downstairs and snipped it to shreds, *while we waited*.

I glanced at Bess and I could see her putting this all together as I did. "Creepy," she breathed.

"Supercreepy," I agreed.

"I can't believe this!" a sharp voice cried out from the door, and we all turned to watch a very upset-looking Akinyi storm into the shop. "This is the worst day ever!"

Syd, whose crying had slowed down considerably, dabbed at her eye with a hankie and shook her head. "No, Akinyi," she said resolutely. "It's definitely a set-back, but I'll be okay."

Akinyi frowned, looking even more annoyed, and then finally her gaze fell on the dress, still draped over the sales girl's arms, and her eyes widened. "Oh my gosh!" she cried. "Syd, what happened to your dress?"

Syd looked puzzled. "It got *slashed*," she replied, "Obviously. What were you yelling about, if not that?"

Akinyi sighed, closed her eyes, and rubbed her temples. "Well, this is a banner day," she snarked, the corners of her lips turning down. "Josh broke up with me."

"What?" Syd asked. "When?"

"Just now," Akinyi replied with a rueful smirk, "on the phone. He's packing his bags to go back to New York right now. We're totally over."

"Why?" Syd asked with a frown. I could tell she was still concerned about her dress and the text, but she also wanted to be there for her friend.

Akinyi shook her head as if to clear it. "Never mind," she said after a little pause. "Let's talk about your dress, and what you're going to do. Are you okay, Syd?"

Everyone began gathering around Sydney, offering their condolences and ideas for getting a new dress. I could also hear some questions about the text she'd received, and what was really going on with the wedding saboteur—was it true Candy wasn't the only one trying to sabotage this wedding?

Tempting as it was to join the crew and see how everyone reacted, I turned to my trusty friends instead. "Okay," I began. "You, me, Deb, Ellie, and Syd have been in the dressing room the whole time—none of us could have slashed the dress. Let's talk about the others."

"Well, Akinyi," Bess suggested, looking unsure. "She was 'outside' for a long time. But she really does seem upset about the breakup—so maybe she really was on the phone with Josh the whole morning?"

I nodded grimly. "Maybe. I think she's definitely a suspect, though. And Pandora disappeared for awhile—though she says she was meditating."

George snorted. "Meditating, schmeditating. I got up to get some water from the cooler in front about fifteen minutes ago, and she was out there on her cell phone. Unless she meditates with a partner, over the phone, I think she was lying."

I sighed. "Great," I replied. "Is anyone *not* a suspect?"

Bess shrugged. "Well, Deb," she replied. "And Ellie. Though she did go out to the car to get her purse at one point… I guess she could have done it then."

I sighed, rubbing my temples.

George pulled her lips into a tight line. "Another thing," she began, clearly about to impart bad news. "We don't know if there's a back entrance to this place."

I looked up at her. Of course! With all my sleuthing experience, how could I have forgotten back entrances?

"Excuse me," I said, gently tugging on the sleeve of the sales clerk, who was still holding the ruined dress as the rest of the bridal party chattered nearby. "Is there a rear entrance to this store?"

The girl nodded. "Sure. But it's not a public entrance."

I glanced back at Bess and George. "But was it locked this morning?"

The girl looked uncomfortable, gently stroking the ruined dress with one hand. "No," she said finally, quietly. "Many of our seamstresses enter that way. And it seems someone did forget to lock the door behind them."

I nodded, trying to communicate with my eyes that I wasn't upset with her. "Thanks for telling me that." I stepped away, turning back to Bess and George.

"Great," said Bess with a sigh. "The field gets even wider."

"So basically *anyone's* a suspect," George agreed. "Everyone except the three of us and Syd."

Bess glanced at me with a playful look. "Well, I don't know," she murmured. "Nancy *did* go to use the restroom that one time."

I shook my head at her. "You came with me!"

"Okay." Bess laughed. "I guess, yes, we can rule out the three of us and Syd."

"And we did narrow down the suspects from the photo," I reminded them. "So really, the only potential wedding saboteur who might have snuck in through the back door is Dragon."

Bess and George suddenly got very focused looks on their faces, looking directly behind me, and I knew someone from the wedding party was coming.

"Well, girls," said Sydney, reaching out to touch my shoulder, "I guess we're done here. You can go home."

I looked up. Behind Syd, the camera crew seemed to have shut down, and was packing up to leave the shop. I looked at our lovely bride-to-be, whose eyes were rimmed with bright, angry red. "I'm so sorry, Syd."

Syd just shrugged sadly, looking away. "I've gotten used to a lot of surprises going ahead with this wedding," she said quietly. "I really loved that dress"— here her voice broke a little—"but the important thing is that I'm marrying Vic. Whoever this wedding saboteur is, he or she can't change that."

"That's a good attitude," Bess enthused, reaching out to squeeze Syd's shoulder.

"I'm sure we'll find another dress," Syd said, but her tone sounded as though she didn't quite believe it. "Anyway, we need to get everyone back to the hotel. Can anyone fit Akinyi, Deb, and Pandora in her car?"

I didn't wait for anyone else to volunteer. "I can!" I cried, a little too loudly. Thank goodness, Bess and George had come in George's car. And the drive back to the hotel would give me plenty of time to get some details on what the rest of the bridal party was doing.

"This is all just so *upsetting*," Pandora said with a sigh, furiously rubbing a pink crystal that she'd pulled out of her purse. "I just can't get over the negative emotions I have associated with this wedding. I have this horrible feeling it's going to get worse before it gets better."

Deb, who was sitting right behind Pandora, giggled nervously. "Oh, come on!" she cried. "Don't be such a Debbie Downer. This has been a tough morning, sure, but . . ." She trailed off, seeming to have trouble coming up with anything positive to say.

"But what?" Akinyi asked from the seat behind me. "Every cloud has a silver lining? April showers bring May flowers? I got it, Deb—and thanks, but I'm just going to go ahead and be sad for the time being."

Deb cringed, clearly hurt by Akinyi's harsh tone. "I'm sorry," she said quickly. "Are you upset about Josh?"

Akinyi snorted, looking out the window. "You *think*?" she asked sarcastically.

"Akinyi," I broke in, trying to use soothing tones to relieve the tension in the car, "do you want to talk about what happened with Josh? I mean, of course you don't have to talk about it if you don't want to, but . . . maybe it would help you feel better?" *And maybe it would help me solve this case,* I added silently.

Akinyi frowned, shaking her head and looking down into her lap. As we stopped at a light and she raised her head again, I could see tears forming at the corners of her eyes. "It's so silly," she said, sniffling. "Basically, he was jealous."

"Of what?" I asked, at the same time Pandora asked, "Of who?"

"Of *Jamal*," Akinyi replied, as though the mere thought were ridiculous. "Can you even?"

I frowned, not sure where she was going with this. "Why would Josh be jealous of Jamal?" I asked. "Had he flirted with you?"

Akinyi smirked ruefully. "No. Worse than that," she replied, then sighed. "Jamal and I were together for a couple weeks last October, while Josh and I were broken up."

My mouth dropped open, and I forgot to go when the light turned green. After a couple steady honks from behind me, I shook my head and got on my way.

They were together? I didn't even know they knew each other!

"How did you meet Jamal?" I asked.

"Syd and Vic introduced us," Akinyi replied. "Jamal was on personal leave, and he came by our apartment for a dinner party Syd and Vic decided to throw. Josh and I had just broken up over some stupid e-mail, and I thought Jamal was really cute and intelligent, so . . ." She threw up her hands in a motion that seemed to say, *That was that.*

"Wow!" cried Deb. She sounded so excited, I thought she might end up in Akinyi's lap. "You and Jamal! Who would have guessed, right?"

Pandora was turned around in her seat, still stroking her crystal as she gazed at Akinyi with a curious expression. "How did you leave it?" she asked. "You know, when Jamal went back to Iraq?"

Akinyi shrugged. "We enjoyed each other's company, and now it's over," she replied. "A week later Josh and I were back together. I never should have told him about Jamal. Ever since then, he's had this complex about my still being into him."

"Did you keep in touch?" I asked.

Akinyi shook her head. "No. He wrote me a couple e-mails, but I was back with Josh, so I didn't answer. But then at the party . . ." She sighed and broke off.

Deb was watching her with wide eyes. "What?!" she demanded. "What! Tell us, Akinyi, what happened?"

Akinyi looked thoughtful, and a tiny smile appeared on her face. "Jamal pulled me aside," she replied. "I went upstairs to use the ladies' room, and he saw me and took me outside. He told me he thought about me all the time, and he thought there might still be something between us."

"Oh my gosh!" Deb cried, bouncing up and down in her chair. "And then? You said?"

Akinyi's expression turned sad again. "I told him no," she replied, "because I really loved Josh. And I did! I mean, I do." She closed her eyes and let out a little sob. Deb leaned over and wrapped her arms around Akinyi, and Akinyi looked horrified and grateful at the same time.

Beside me, Pandora was watching all of this with a pensive expression. "It can be hard sometimes," she said finally, reaching over to press her pink crystal into Akinyi's hand. "I know how it goes. Sometimes it can be hard to let go, even though a relationship is over."

Hmmmm.

I pulled into the hotel parking lot, considering all the new information I now had to think about.

REALITY TELEVISION?

The *Daredevils* producers wasted no time in setting up a day for Syd to shop for a new dress with her bridal party. That Thursday morning, just two days after I'd dropped Akinyi, Deb, and Pandora back at the hotel, Bess, George, and I traveled back there to board a limo filled with bridesmaids, both moms—and a camera crew.

"Try to act natural," Hans encouraged us, obviously trying very hard not to scowl at our totally unnatural behavior. Deb had just sidled up to Sydney, smiled, looked directly into the camera, and announced in a near-shout, "SO, SYDNEY, TELL US ABOUT THE DRESS YOU WANT TO BUY."

I understood that Hans wanted us to act "real," but it was difficult with eight women, a cameraman, a sound man, Donald, and Hans crammed into a stretch limo. On the phone last night, Donald had explained to me that we'd spend the whole day traveling from bridal shop to bridal shop, trying to find Syd the perfect replacement dress in just a few hours. Now Donald watched us with a concerned expression, no doubt worried about how this "scene" was going to turn out.

Bess took a small bite of a doughnut and settled back against the leather bench, clearly trying to act calm. "What are you looking for, Syd?" she asked in a tone that closely matched her normal voice.

Syd sighed, looking thoughtful. Of all of us, she was the most comfortable around the cameras—probably from all the practice she'd had this week! "I think, now that I have a chance to start over, I want to go all-out," she replied. "Like a ball gown! I think something big and poufy could be fun."

George caught her eye and shook her head with a faux grimace. "I can't believe we're related," she deadpanned.

Syd just chuckled. "You can do it your way when *you* walk down the aisle, coz."

Soon we reached the first store, where we all trooped out and set up in the dressing room to watch

Syd try on five dresses the producers had already picked out. Syd liked a couple of them, but each dress seemed to have a problem associated with it—it was too big, or it couldn't be delivered in time, or the sample dress (which Syd would have to take, since she was buying on short notice) was way too big for Syd's birdlike frame.

"Don't you think it's weird," George whispered to me during a break in filming, "that the producers already picked these dresses out, and yet they won't be ready in time?"

I shrugged. Even just in the last couple of hours, I'd developed a lot of skepticism about so-called "reality" TV. The shopping was taking forever, because some dresses had to be tried on several times so the cameraman could get shots from several different angles. If Syd said something interesting and the sound guy didn't pick it up, she had to say it again—and again. And again. If she didn't sound "natural" enough on the second or third or sixteenth take, Hans would rephrase it for her. And the whole time, Donald was pushing the rest of us to "get involved."

"Do you think this is the right dress for her?" he whispered to Ellie as Syd modeled a low-cut number the producers had picked out for her. "Would you feel comfortable with her wearing that on her wedding day?"

Ellie had looked incredibly uncomfortable, but had finally said diplomatically, "I think she looks very pretty." No matter what anyone asked, she wouldn't say any more.

We traveled to the next store, and then the next. While the producers had selected only a few dresses at each location, it still took forever for Syd to try them all on, due to all the setting up and reshoots. We were all hungry, since we weren't supposed to eat lunch until after we finished three stores, and I could sense everyone growing tired of shopping. It didn't help, of course, that none of the dresses the producers had chosen actually seemed suitable.

Finally the final dress was filmed, and Vic's mom seemed to please Hans by telling Syd it was a little tight. Syd chuckled, and we all perked up a little, assuming this meant we could leave the store and have lunch. But then Donald announced that Hans was going to do one-on-one interviews, starting with the moms. He pulled them into a separate room as Syd dropped next to me on the sofa with a sigh.

I waited until the full crew was out of earshot before turning to her with an incredulous look. "*How* have you put up with this all week?!" I demanded.

Syd just laughed. "Oh, Nance," she said, squeezing my arm. "I'm sorry, you guys. I know this is tough. Being a reality TV star isn't all it's cracked up to be!"

I shook my head. "No, no. We're fine. This is just one long day for us, but you've been doing this since you arrived in town! You must be going nuts."

Syd leaned back against the sofa and shrugged. "It's not fun, sometimes. But ever since I took Vic back, I have a new philosophy."

George leaned in. "Which is?"

Syd smiled. "I love Vic," she replied. "And I'm getting married to him, and that's all that matters."

Akinyi moved closer, shaking her head. "Still," she said irritably, "don't you ever regret agreeing to get married on television? I mean, I would get sick of these guys following me around, making me re-enact everything so they can film it in the right light."

Syd frowned, looking thoughtful. "Well, you know, I was originally against it," she replied. *Yes—you* and *your mom,* I thought. "But when I did the math I realized Vic was right. Filming the whole thing might be a little uncomfortable, but in the end, we'll have a great DVD to show our kids and a nice little nest egg to start out with!"

Akinyi raised an eyebrow. "How *much* of a nest egg?" she demanded. "Because I'm telling you, I would want to be able to quit my job to put up with as much as you're putting up with."

I could sense everyone squirming uncomfortably. Granted, Akinyi was still dealing with her very sudden breakup, but she seemed to get more irritable and cranky every day. And asking Syd exactly how much she and Vic were getting for this special seemed a little impolite.

Syd didn't look upset, though. "Let's put it this way," she explained. "Vic and I will be able to put a down payment on a nice house—and have enough left over to throw a whole other wedding, if we want."

Akinyi looked skeptical. "Okay," she replied, turning away. "If that's enough for you."

I saw a little crease form between Syd's eyebrows. It looked like her friend's criticisms were finally starting to get to her. "Listen," she said, "the producers have been very generous. They're giving us a nice lump sum, plus they're paying for the wedding, paying for the honeymoon, they wrote that nice check for the Books for Kids Foundation—"

But then Syd broke off, putting her hand over her mouth, as though she realized she'd said something she shouldn't.

"Huh?" Bess asked. "What's the Books for Kids Foundation?"

Syd glanced over at the door to the room where the mothers were being interviewed, then lowered her voice. "I'm really not supposed to say anything about this," she whispered, "but the producers wrote a nice check to my mother's favorite charity,

Books for Kids. That really changed her perception of them, and of whether this TV special was a good idea."

I met George's eye. *Aaaaahhh.* That explained Ellie's sudden turnaround—and her ambivalence about the whole TV issue, especially when her daughter was threatened.

"Isn't that a lot of money?" Deb asked, tilting her head. "It must be expensive for them to film, too. It seems like the producers are spending an awful lot to get this special."

Syd shrugged. "It seems that way to you and me, but in television, this is just a drop in the bucket," she explained. "It's still much cheaper for them to produce than scripted television. And they're expecting great ratings, since Vic is so popular."

Hmmm. I leaned back on the sofa, thinking this over. So Ellie really had no motive to stop the wedding—not like it had seemed particularly likely in the first place. That left Dragon, Akinyi, and Pandora.

One down, three to go.

"But what do you *really* think?" Syd asked us all three hours later, casting an annoyed glance at the cameraman. We were at our last bridal store, and Syd was on her last dress, a champagne-colored, mermaid-shaped gown that had a bodice dripping with heavy, sparkling beads. Hans had just verified with the shop owner that this gown could be ready by Saturday—and in Syd's size.

"I think . . . I think . . . it's nice," Ellie said nervously, glancing over at the camera. Everyone seemed uncomfortable speaking up. This dress seemed to be the total opposite of what Syd was looking for—but it was here, and it was the only passable dress we'd seen that could be ready for the wedding in two days.

Syd sighed, looking in the mirror again. "You don't think it makes me look too old?" she asked.

Nobody answered.

"Mom?" Syd prodded.

Ellie sighed, shaking her head. "Oh, Sydney," she said wearily, "don't you like it? It's your opinion that matters."

We were all tired at the end of the day, and it seemed to me that almost everyone was a little on edge. Personally, I thought the dress *did* look old on Syd, but I didn't want to say anything in case she liked it, or her mother liked it. I figured their opinions were more important.

Syd turned back around and looked right at Akinyi, who was examining her fingernails, looking bored.

"Akinyi," Syd said in a pointed tone. "Wasn't there

something you wanted to do here? Something . . . wacky?"

Akinyi looked up and met Syd's eyes. Immediately, I saw something pass between them—some kind of understanding. "Oh, um, yes!" Akinyi replied. "I, um, I . . ." She trailed off, looking around the room. Then suddenly she looked back at Syd. "I challenge you to a dress-off!"

Syd broke into a grin. "A dress-off?" she asked. "And what's that?"

Akinyi stood, seeming to be working something out in her own head. "It means I'll try on some dresses," she replied, "and we'll see who looks better!" She began walking toward the main showroom. "I just need to find some dresses that suit me!"

On her way out, she glanced at Donald and Hans and cleared her throat loudly. Donald gave Hans a pointed look, gesturing to the cameraman. "Hans?" he asked.

Hans thought for a minute, then sighed and nodded. "Yes, let's get this," he agreed. The three then followed Akinyi out into the showroom, followed by the sound man.

Syd turned back to all of us. "Okay," she said. "What do you *really* think?"

We all looked at each other, surprised.

"It *does* look kind of old, Syd," Bess admitted.

"Yeah," agreed Pandora.

Deb nodded, lips pursed. "I hate to criticize your taste, Syd," she said, giggling nervously, "but . . . um . . ."

Syd sighed, abruptly unzipping the dress and stepping out of it. "No, you're absolutely right," she agreed. "This isn't the dress I want to get married in." She grabbed the simple wrap dress she'd worn that day and slipped it on.

"But Syd," Ellie said, her eyes full of sympathy, "what will you do? What dress will you get married in? I can't believe we didn't find something today."

Syd shrugged. "I don't know, Mom. I just have to believe something will work out. If I don't find another bridal gown, well—" She grinned. "—I guess I'll just marry Vic in my old bathrobe. It's not the dress that's important, anyway."

I smiled. "That was a pretty cool trick, Syd," I said, nodding my head in the direction of the showroom. "Sending Akinyi out there to distract the camera."

Syd chuckled, looking a little embarrassed to be caught. "You like that, huh?" she asked. "Vic taught me that. He actually tried to use it the other night, at the—um—bachelor party." She flashed an uncomfortable look at Pandora. "When—you know—when the photo was snapped, he tried to send Dragon out to climb the flagpole and distract the camera crew." Her smile faded. "Of course, that didn't work."

He tried to send Dragon out . . . I gasped. So that explained why Dragon wasn't in the photo! He hadn't taken it or sent it . . . he had simply been sent outside by Vic to distract the crew.

I glanced at George, but she was looking at Syd, smiling encouragingly. "I guess you've perfected it," she said, and Syd smiled again.

"Yeah," she said with a little chuckle, "if you've got camera crews following you around twenty-four/seven, it's good to have an escape plan!"

At that moment, Akinyi strode back into the dressing room, followed closely by Hans and the cameraman. "Oh, never mind," she said breezily, winking at Syd before the cameraman could catch up. "I didn't see anything I liked. You win this round, Syd."

Hans trailed into the room, and took notice of Syd wearing her street clothes again. "So that was a no?" he asked. "You decided not to go with the last dress?"

Syd shook her head.

"What will you wear?" Hans asked, as the cameraman trained his camera on Syd.

Syd shrugged, looking totally unconcerned. "I'll find something," she promised. "Even if I have to wear sweatpants."

Hans nodded. "Well, I don't think you'll have to do that. *Julie?*" He raised his voice, calling back into the showroom. "*Julie?* Do you have something to say to our blushing bride?"

A petite Latina stepped into the dressing room, almost dwarfed by the huge, billowing dress she carried in her hands. Immediately the cameraman focused on her.

"Sydney," she announced, smiling at our bride, "our store, Julie's Ultimate Bridal, would like to donate this beautiful Hilda Reynolds dress to you for your wedding."

Bess gasped. "Hilda Reynolds!" she whispered to me. "Her dresses go for up to ten thousand dollars!"

Syd looked very touched, and as she touched the dress, which she called "perfect," she broke down and began to cry. "Oh, thank you," she said, hugging Julie. "This is my dream dress! I never would have thought I'd find something so beautiful on such short notice!"

Everyone crowded around to examine the dress—which really *was* gorgeous—congratulate Syd, and thank Julie. After a few minutes Hans announced that Syd would have to stay at the store for a last-minute fitting, but everyone else would be taking the limo back to the hotel.

It took a few minutes to get everything together, and as we filed out, I noticed Hans talking on a cell phone just inside the front door of the store.

"Oh, it went perfectly," he said with a chuckle. "She even squeezed out some tears! You were right about keeping her out and busy all day—I think that frustration really got us an amazing reaction. It will look great on film."

My mouth dropped open and I turned to find Bess and George, but they were already climbing in to the limo. I'd realized over the course of the day that "reality TV" was a bit of a misnomer—clearly the producers manipulated peoples' reactions a bit, and set up the action as they saw fit. But this entire day had been a setup to get the perfect shot of Syd crying over her dress? All of our time had been wasted—and all of our emotions toyed with? I felt a little sick.

Then a crazy thought occurred to me: could *Hans* be the wedding saboteur? Was it possible that the producers of *Daredevils* were sabotaging the wedding themselves, just to get the most dramatic special possible?

"No, no," Hans was saying now, glancing back toward the dressing room and Syd. "She's fine now. And no further incidents, thank goodness. We're all safe here."

Immediately I felt a little silly. Okay, Hans and his crew had manipulated us to get good television: that was, after all, their job. But clearly they wouldn't commit a crime for ratings. No reputable TV company would do that.

I pulled myself together and headed for the limo.

I had a lot to think over.

7

HEART OF GLASS

"Is anyone else nervous?" Bess asked as I pulled my Prius into the parking lot for Kelley Park, the gorgeous, sprawling nature preserve where Syd and Vic were to be married the next day. It was Friday night, the night of the wedding rehearsal and rehearsal dinner. It should have been a night for eager celebration, but given everything that had happened to Vic and Syd over the last few weeks, I think we were all feeling concerned about what else the wedding saboteur had up his or her sleeve.

"I am," I admitted. "But I also feel like we're getting closer to a culprit. Now that Ellie and Dragon have been pretty much cleared, we're down to Pandora, Akinyi—and Jamal."

"Jamal?" George asked, looking confused. "I thought we cleared him when we realized he wasn't here for the first few attacks."

I nodded, but held up my index finger as I clarified, "That was *before* we found out he had a fling with Akinyi." I gave my friends a meaningful look.

"You mean they might have been working together?" Bess asked.

"Exactly." I turned off the car and sat for a moment, sighing, thinking of all I had to figure out before tomorrow. "I just wish I could figure out a motivation for Akinyi and Jamal."

George frowned. "Yeah, that's hard to imagine. It's the best man and the maid of honor—why would they want to stop the wedding?"

I shrugged. "Unless something happened between them and the happy couple that we don't know about."

"Akinyi *has* been pretty irritable," Bess pointed out.

George nodded. "True," she admitted. Then a mischievous smile appeared on her lips. "But then again, she's a model. Maybe she's just hungry."

I groaned. "George!" I chided, as Bess elbowed her cousin in the ribs. "Jokes, not helping!"

George shrugged, still smiling. "I couldn't resist," she said. "And you know who else is hungry? Me, right now. Let's get this rehearsal started so we can eat."

Nervous as I was, I couldn't argue with her.

At the small beach that allowed residents to swim in a calm part of the river, the *Daredevils* crew had set up a white trellis that would be covered in roses for the actual ceremony, fronted with hundreds of white wooden chairs. Set dressers were busily adorning each chair with rich satin ribbons in the deep rose color Syd had chosen for her bridesmaid gowns, and a huge lighting crew was working on rigging up a complicated system of lights. A few crew members were lounging up by the trellis: cameramen, sound men, lighting guys, and a neurotic-looking Donald, who was walking in circles, flipping through a clipboard. They were no doubt waiting for the bride- and groom-to-be to arrive. Most of the wedding party and family were there already, milling around and waiting.

Akinyi was sitting on one of the white seats, impatiently checking her watch. "They're ten minutes late," she announced to anyone listening. "Why don't we ever start filming on time?"

Smoothly Jamal stepped over from the small cluster of crew members he'd been chatting up. "Why, are you in a hurry to get back to the hotel, Miss Thang?" he asked with a sly smile. "Do you have a hot date tonight?"

For a moment anger flashed in Akinyi's eyes, and I wondered if she was going to snap back at him. But then her face suddenly relaxed, and she seemed to realize how cranky she'd sounded. "Maybe I do," she said jokingly, her cheeks reddening just a bit. "Or maybe I'm just eager to get this show on the road so my best friend can get married already."

Jamal smiled again, warmly, and settled close in the seat next to Akinyi. "I can identify with that," he said. Then he moved his head close to hers and dropped his voice low, so low that I couldn't hear what he was saying.

At that moment George walked up and pinched me.

"Ouch!" I cried.

"You might want to remember to blink every once in a while," she said, following my gaze over to the best man and maid of honor. "It's a little obvious you're spying when your jaw is on the ground like that."

I smiled sheepishly. "Do you think anyone noticed?"

George shook her head. "I think those two are in a world of their own," she observed.

"It is interesting," I suggested quietly, "that Akinyi's letting him flirt so much when she said she was so torn up over her break up with Josh."

George shrugged. "Or maybe she really does miss Josh, but she's attracted to Jamal too. It can happen sometimes."

Trying to be less conspicuous, I chanced another glance in Akinyi's direction. Now the two of them were giggling, heads still close. I watched as Jamal lightly touched Akinyi's knee, then quickly pulled his hand away.

"Or maybe," I suggested to George, "they've been hiding their relationship all this time! Maybe they *are* working together and Akinyi staged the breakup the other day to distract us from the fact that she could have shredded the dress!"

George watched Akinyi and Jamal for a few seconds before shaking her head. "Honestly, Nance," she said, "if you weren't right so often I'd think you were nuts."

I narrowed my eyes, watching as Jamal touched Akinyi's shoulder before walking back to the crew. "It's either them or Pandora."

Just then I heard a rumble going through the crowd, and I turned to see a limo pull up to the park entrance. After a few seconds the passenger door opened and Vic's mom got out, followed by Syd's dad, Ellie, and then Vic. Vic smiled when he realized everyone was watching him—even giving a quick "finger-gun" salute to the cameras, which had started filming. But as he stepped away and Syd gingerly stepped out, I was stunned to see that she was wiping away tears.

"Oh my gosh," whispered Bess, moving over to where George and I stood. "Maybe the wedding saboteur struck again while we weren't around!"

The crowd seemed to politely back away once they realized Syd was upset, and soon the low din of wedding party members talking amongst themselves rose up, and someone from the crew started playing classical music over the huge sound system they'd installed. I was about to say something to answer Bess, but then I spotted Syd moving in our direction, quickly followed by camera and sound guys.

Vic stepped up behind her, touching her arm, but Syd angrily pulled away. "Don't start!" she barked, moving quickly to join our small group.

"Hey," George said warmly, placing a hand on her cousin's shoulder. "You okay? Did something happen?"

Syd's eyes were rimmed with red. "Did something happen? Yeah, something happened all right. Vic told me that if we get married and something happens to him, he wants me to remarry!"

Syd bugged out her eyes, like the ridiculousness of

this request was obvious. But George, Bess, and I just looked at each other blankly, until finally recognition flashed in Bess's eyes and she announced in a relieved voice, "Oh! You two just had a fight!"

"Ahhh," George and I murmured, unable to hide our own relief.

"So you're okay?" I asked. "No acid in your shower, no poison in your coffee this morning?"

Syd looked at me like I was nuts. *"Okay?"* she asked. "No, I am *not* okay. I just had a huge fight with the man I'm going to spend the rest of my life with! Over a *hugely* important issue! He doesn't even love me enough to want me to stay true to him once he's dead! Don't you *get* it?"

We all looked at Syd, clearly not getting it.

"Um," Bess began softly, taking Syd's hand, "maybe it actually shows how much Vic *does* love you? You know, that he wants you to be happy?"

Syd glared at her. *"I can't believe you're taking his side!"*

Just then, thank goodness, Ellie approached from behind, dragging a chastened and very nervous-looking Vic. "Sydney," she said gently. "Why don't you two just talk to each other and work this out? Remember, you're both very tense right now. This is a stressful night for you both. Maybe you could be a bit easier on each other?"

Syd looked from her mom to Vic, and slowly her

face crumpled. "Oh, Vic, I'm sorry!" she cried, sniffling. "I never meant . . . I just wanted . . ."

Ellie nodded, gesturing for them to talk alone a little ways away. "Yes, yes. You two work it out."

Syd and Vic hugged and walked away together, into the privacy of a few trees. The crew members that had come with Syd quickly moved away to follow them. Ellie looked at the three of us and sighed. "My husband and I had a *huge* fight the night before our wedding," she explained. "All those nerves, you know? I remember throwing a vase he'd given me out our third-story window. And oddly enough, I can't remember what we were fighting about."

Bess nodded seriously. "Are they nervous about another attack?"

Ellie's face turned more serious, and she nodded. "Of course," she replied. "I just wish I could make it all better for them. But yes, given everything that's happened so far . . ."

We all nodded sympathetically. It seemed so unfair for Syd and Vic to have such a crazy threat hanging over their wedding day. I just hoped something would happen tonight that would be enough to lead me to the culprit!

Even though the wedding rehearsal was only expected to take about twenty minutes, it was over an hour before we made it to Chez Philippe, the fancy French restaurant where the *Daredevils* producers had planned the rehearsal dinner. Inside, hundreds of candles illuminated a cozy, pink-hued private room. Four tables of six ringed a tiny two-person table for Syd and Vic. Bess, George, and I headed right to our table, which, once again, we were sharing with Akinyi, Deb, and Pandora.

"*That* was a disaster," George muttered under her breath, shaking her head as she put down her things.

"I know," Bess chimed in. "Syd and Vic were a mess! Even after they made up, it was like they were too rattled to get through it."

"They couldn't even get the vows right when the minister had them doing one word at a time," I agreed with a sigh. "I just hope they get some good rest tonight, so they can focus better tomorrow."

Gradually the whole group trickled in, and finally Syd and Vic entered, followed by the camera crew, and smiling sheepishly as they made their way to their private table.

"Everyone," Vic announced, raising his glass, "I'm so sorry our nerves made the rehearsal go so long tonight. It's just that I love this girl so much, and I'm so . . . so . . ." His voice cracked, and he turned to face his bride-to-be. Syd smiled encouragingly and squeezed his arm, and he continued: "So happy to be marrying her! So thank you, everyone, for coming and supporting us tonight."

After the happy couple sat down, Vic's mom rose and gave a short speech, saying how excited she was to watch her son marry such a wonderful girl and how pleased she was to be here with all their loved ones. When she sat down, everyone applauded her, and then the waiters appeared to serve the soup.

Akinyi turned to the rest of us at the table, looking curious. "Why did *she* just make a speech?"

Pandora, who had been staring off at a point on the other side of the room, perked up. "It's this ancient patriarchal tradition that the bride's family pays for the wedding, but the groom's family pays for the rehearsal dinner. It's really sexist, actually."

"Yeah, but the *Daredevils* producers are paying for everything in this case. Right?" asked Akinyi. When no one responded, she looked around the table and repeated, "Right?"

"Right," I said with a shrug, hoping to change the subject. It felt a little awkward to be talking about who paid for the wedding as we all sat there enjoying it. "So . . . um . . . what kind of shoes is everyone wearing tomorrow?"

Bess shot me an amazed glance, and I shrugged at her. I knew she must find it extremely out of character for Nancy Drew, penny loafer aficionado, to ask about anything shoe-related, but I just wanted to change the subject.

George shrugged, tearing off a piece of bread. "Silver flats for me. Picked out by my super fashionable cousin." She elbowed Bess.

"Me too," Bess agreed. "And Nancy, your shoes are similar."

Deb leaned in, widening her eyes. "I got the *prettiest* shoes at Penney's," she said in a confidential tone. "They're white, high-heeled, with a little strap."

Akinyi looked dubious. "I brought some couture heels I got from a designer," she said in a bored tone, as next to me, Bess's jaw dropped to the table. Akinyi turned to Pandora, whose gaze was still fixed across the room. She seemed a million miles away. "Pandora? Pandora? Did you hear us? What shoes are you wearing?"

Pandora didn't respond, and I followed the direction of her gaze to see what she was looking at. When I realized what it was, I almost gasped. Syd and Vic! For at least half the time we'd been sitting at our table, Pandora had been intently watching Syd and Vic at *their* table—taking in their each and every move.

Pandora smiled a little and waved, but when I looked at Syd and Vic, they didn't seem to notice. By the time I turned back to Pandora, she was frowning.

She turned back to her soup in front of her and fiddled with the spoon.

"Pandora?" Akinyi was still asking. "Earth to Pandora!"

Pandora looked up, not looking terribly interested. "Yes?"

"What's *wrong* with you?" Akinyi asked, shaking her head. "You're like a million miles away. Are you feeling all right?"

Pandora looked back down at her soup, sighing deeply. "It's the wedding," she said sadly. "I just still have this terrible feeling. I can't believe Vic doesn't sense it. He's usually so in tune with the universe."

Hmmm. I leaned in, trying to get Pandora's attention. "If you were Vic, what would you do?" I asked.

Pandora looked up at me. "Cancel the wedding," she replied quickly, with a *well, duh* expression. "Before someone gets hurt!"

Akinyi watched Pandora, her lips slowly forming a skeptical smirk. "Before someone gets hurt?" she asked. "Or before the guy you're not over marries someone else?"

Pandora looked up, anger flashing in her eyes. It made me realize that, up until that point, I'd never seen Pandora look truly upset. "You don't know what you're talking about," she said in a dark, low voice. "Excuse me. I need to meditate." And she stood up from the table, walked out of the room, and was gone.

Akinyi just watched her go, shaking her head. "I'm so tired of her bringing everyone down," she explained to the rest of us. "She needs to get over Vic, and fast."

I didn't know what to say. My two prime suspects were fighting with each other. Pandora *did* seem awfully obsessed with Vic tonight—but what did that mean? Nothing had happened to either Syd *or* Vic since the dress slashing, and the wedding was almost here.

Bess elbowed me. "Okay, I think I've seen enough excitement tonight," she whispered. "Let's hurry up and eat before something else happens!"

I dug into my food, although I realized I didn't have much of an appetite. I was having my own wedding jitters. Not about getting married myself, obviously—but that the night would continue without anything happening, and then I wouldn't catch the wedding saboteur, and he or she would do something awful at the wedding.

The salad and the entrees were served without incident. It wasn't until the dessert course was served—a decadent, gooey molten chocolate cake that everyone at our table was enjoying *immensely*, even Pandora—that a loud *clink* could be heard over the din of conversation.

At the sweetheart table, Syd and Vic were frowning as Vic dug into his cake. "What the . . . ?" he asked, carefully pulling the cake apart. He gasped and held something up on his fork.

I leaned in close to see, as the crowd gasped. It was several shards of glass!

I jumped out of my seat. "Vic!" I cried. "Don't move! Don't eat that! Let me see!"

I ran over, and Vic handed me his fork. Putting it down and digging into the cake with his knife, I could see several other jagged pieces—small enough to be swallowed without his noticing it, but large enough to do some serious internal damage.

"Oh my gosh," cried Sydney, her eyes welling up with tears. "Vic, oh no. It's not over. He's struck again!"

Just then, we all heard a loud *beep*. I looked at Syd, both of our faces drooping with recognition. Syd reached down and pulled her PDA out of her bag, then wordlessly showed the screen to me.

PREPARE FOR ALL UR DREAMS 2 B SHATTERED.

8

SECRET VISITS

Syd was inconsolable. I tried my best to comfort her—at least Vic hadn't taken a bite! At least he found the glass before it could do any damage!—but nothing seemed to make her feel any better.

"If this was the wedding saboteur's plan for the rehearsal dinner, Nancy," she told me between sobs, "imagine what he has on deck for tomorrow!"

It was true. What worried me most about the glass incident was that it proved to us the wedding saboteur was still at large—and still fundamentally opposed to this wedding. And whoever this person was, he or she had proven that they were willing to see someone get hurt, even killed, just as long as it kept Vic and Syd from becoming husband and wife.

"I'll catch him, Syd," I told the very jittery bride-to-be. "I promise you." But the truth is, I'm not even sure she heard me over her crying.

"What's up?" asked George as I returned to our table.

"Syd's pretty upset," I replied.

George nodded grimly. "Bess and I checked with the kitchen staff," she told me. "The producers have really been on them to make sure the food they serve is safe. The chef said Vic and Syd's food was checked and rechecked before it left the kitchen—there's no way someone inserted the glass back there."

I nodded grimly. "And they were at the table almost the whole time the desserts were sitting there," I added. "Except . . ."

"Except!" Bess cried excitedly. "Right when the chocolate cakes were put down, Syd and Vic were over at my mom's table, talking to Ellie."

I nodded. "That's right," I said, remembering. After the desserts were put down, I vaguely recalled Syd and Vic rushing back to their table to try them. "They weren't gone long, though. Maybe a couple of minutes?"

Bess nodded. "Just enough time to for someone to come up and mess with Vic's cake—right?"

I sighed. It was hard to imagine someone from the rehearsal dinner—someone Vic and Syd loved—trying to hurt them during the happiest time of their lives. But it was hard to argue with reality. Unless it was someone from the *Daredevils* crew? I briefly flashed back to Hans's phone conversation two days before, and my sudden hunch that the producers themselves might be behind the incidents, but even now it seemed crazy to me. Once the glass had been found, the *Daredevils* crew had sprung into action—every crew member not actively working on the filming was sent to question restaurant staff, talk to the police, and comfort Syd. And they'd been amping up security with every new incident. It really seemed like they had the couple's best interests at heart.

Suddenly I realized something. "Akinyi was sitting with us at the table the whole time," I pointed out. "She couldn't have done it."

George nodded. "But Pandora has been up several times to 'meditate,'" she pointed out.

"And Jamal," Bess added sadly, as though it pained her to say it. "I noticed he got up from the groomsmen's table right before the dessert course was served. So it could have been him."

I frowned, looking around the room. Somebody here was the wedding saboteur. But who?

Akinyi and Jamal had gathered around Syd and

Vic's table, and Jamal had his hand on his best friend's shoulder. He seemed to be shaking his head, trying to soothe the couple. Akinyi, meanwhile, had pulled out a lace handkerchief and was drying Syd's eyes. She, too, put her hand on Syd's back, whispering something in her ear and patting. The two certainly looked sincerely concerned for their friends.

I pulled my eyes away. Across the room, at the restaurant entrance, I saw Pandora approaching the glass doors, looking ticked. She slammed her cell phone shut and shoved it in her pocket, shaking her head like she hadn't liked what the person on the other end of the line had had to say. I watched Pandora look around nervously. Her gaze seemed to fall on something she liked, and a quick smile formed on her lips. But just as quickly, she seemed to panic and look away.

All in all, she was looking very neurotic and not Pandora-like *at all*.

I turned back to my friends. "Guys," I said, "I need your help."

Ten minutes later, the three of us were back in my Prius, headed for the Hotel Bristol.

"What did you tell Sydney?" Bess asked me.

"I told her I had a stomachache and you two had agreed to give me a ride home," I replied. "I figure we have about a half-hour window before everyone finishes up and heads back to the hotel. And in that time I'm going to need to check some things out."

"I can't wait!" Bess cried, clapping her hands together excitedly. "It's been too long since I've done any real snooping!"

I glanced at her warily in the rearview mirror. "Uh, Bess . . ."

George smirked, turning to face me from the passenger seat. "Let me guess," she said. "Bess and I are on lobby watch?"

I could see Bess's shoulders fall in the backseat. "Yes," I agreed. "Sorry, Bess. But I need to move superfast, and I'm going to need some warning if any of the rehearsal dinner guests start coming back through the lobby."

Bess just sighed, looking put-upon. "Okay," she agreed. "I guess it's never easy being the best friend of the original supersleuth of River Heights."

George held up her index finger. "*One* of the best friends!" she corrected her cousin. "And I agree—it's not easy. But I'll feel pretty good once we catch the jerk who's trying to ruin Syd's wedding."

Bess smiled. "Agreed," she said.

The Hotel Bristol seemed pretty quiet with the entire wedding party elsewhere. I led Bess and George in through the back door, and then immediately took a back stairway up to the third floor.

"Where are we going?" Bess demanded, looking confused. "The lobby's that way."

"Trust me," I replied, pulling off my jacket and stashing it behind a potted plant in the hallway. "Now, you guys can head to the lobby with me, but you have to act like you're not *with* me. Pretend we're two separate parties."

George looked doubtful, but she knew enough to trust me on matters like these. "Okay," she agreed. "Who are you? Never seen you before in my life."

I led them across the third floor to a set of elevators that I knew led to the lobby. When the elevator arrived, all three of us got on, but Bess and George stood toward the rear of he car, as though we'd never met.

"Once these doors open," I told them in a low voice, "we don't know each other, okay? And you know, if you see anyone, *especially* Pandora, you call me."

Bess nodded, but George furrowed her brows. "Why are you talking to us, stranger?" she asked.

The elevator dinged. "Cute," I muttered, just before the doors opened. Then, putting on my cutest "girl in distress" look, I marched up to the front desk.

"Hi," I said a little sheepishly to the young man who was working reception.

"Hi," he said, smiling warmly. "Can I help you?"

"I sure hope so," I replied, with a little nervous laugh. "See, I just locked myself out of my room. And, unfortunately, I was kind of in the middle of running myself a bath . . ."

The man's face broke out in concern as he realized what I was saying.

"Exactly!" I said, trying to look really embarrassed. "And, unfortunately, I don't have any ID on me, but I'm sure you can understand I *really* need to get back there . . ."

"Of course, of course," the man replied, perking up and typing something into his computer. "We can have one of our security guards bring you up. What is your name?"

I smiled. "Pandora Simmons," I replied.

"Here you go, ma'am," a security guard named Hank told me a few minutes later, as he opened the door to room 238. "Hope we got you up here in time! We haven't heard any complaints of water leaking into the room below . . ."

"Oh, I'm sure it's fine, thanks!" I said with a smile, gently closing the door behind me. The clock on the bedside table said it was 9:12—about fifteen minutes after we'd left the rehearsal dinner. I just hoped everyone was still hanging around and talking, and not running back to the hotel to get a good night's sleep.

Turning on the overhead light, I glanced around the room. I didn't immediately see anything unusual. Pandora's huge vintage suitcase was open on a dresser near the window, and her signature gauzy, brightly-printed clothes spilled out. I could see her bridesmaid dress hanging on a hook on the outside of the closet.

Trying my best to be quiet, I moved to the door to the small hotel bathroom and turned on that light. Glancing around, I gasped—right there, on the vanity, was a broken wine glass! I walked into the bathroom and examined it, not wanting to touch it or get fingerprints on it. But just looking carefully, it seemed that the glass had been shattered and the jagged pieces placed in what remained of the glass bowl. I couldn't be sure, but it definitely seemed possible to me that a few pieces were missing.

"That could be it," I murmured to myself, taking a quick glance around the rest of the bathroom, opening and closing some drawers (which all turned out to be empty). "That could be the glass that was pushed into Vic's dessert."

Hopeful, but not convinced, I walked back out to the main room. I wanted to look at the rest of Pandora's things and see if I could find some more evidence that would support Pandora being the culprit. I dug through her suitcase, but didn't see anything notable. Just a bunch of clothing, crystals, and essential oils.

I looked in the closet, but it was nearly empty. It held only Pandora's bridesmaid dress (on the front) and a skirt she'd worn to the bachelorette party. Walking over to the bed, I glanced at the nightstand. That was where lots of people kept personal items, like books, journals, even photos of loved ones. Pandora's nightstand, though, was curiously empty. *That's odd,* I thought, pulling open the top drawer.

Inside was the standard Bible, put there by the Gideons. But also . . . I reached my hand in further and felt a small, paperbound volume. I pulled it out. *A journal!* And also—my hand hit something cold and sharp. I fished around, and gasped when I saw what it was: a pair of sharp scissors.

Scissors just like the ones that were probably used to slash Syd's dress.

I opened the journal to a recent page and cast my eyes over it:

"Miss him so much it's driving me crazy . . . So hard to be this close to him and not able to touch him . . . But if anyone knew how I really feel, it could ruin everything . . ."

I bit my lip. She had to be talking about Vic!

Looking across the room, I suddenly spotted

something I hadn't noticed on my first pass, because it was covered by a wild paisley scarf. But there, on the round table where hotel guests could set up a mini-office, was a laptop computer.

I ran over to it, flipping it open and touching the spacebar to take it out of sleep mode. When the screen came to life, I quickly moved the mouse over the Internet browser icon and double clicked. . . .

Rrrring! Rrrring!

My heart jumped into my throat as my cell phone began to ring. It had to be Bess and George! Fishing it out of my pocket, I held it to my ear and answered, "Is she in the lobby?"

"Worse," George replied. "We didn't see her come in at first, because she came in a side door. But Bess just caught a glimpse of her coat in the elevator as the doors were closing! Nance, you have to get out of there. She's going to be on the floor any minute!"

But as George said this, I could hear that it was already too late. Loud giggling in the hallway could only be coming from Pandora. And then—a deeper voice. Uh-oh. Pandora was with a *guy*!

"I think we were right to ditch the party. Syd was getting so upset anyway. And we might be able to see each other again."

My heart was pounding in my throat. Throwing the laptop, scarf, and journal back where I'd found them, I launched myself into the bathroom, stumbling into the shower and closing the curtain to hide me. *Please, God, just make Pandora and her date feel nice and clean and* not *in need of a shower!*

As soon as my feet hit the porcelain shower floor, the door to the hotel room opened. I heard more giggling, then a male laugh.

"We made it!" Pandora called happily, and I heard the springs of her bed squeak as she sat down heavily on the mattress.

More laughter followed, and while the two of them were talking, I decided to take a peek. I stepped quietly out of the shower, pulled the bathroom door closer to me, and silently peered around it to see—

Pandora and *Dragon* sitting on the bed!

PAST GRIEVANCES

"It's been so hard these past couple of weeks, trying to pretend like I care that Vic is getting married," Pandora told Dragon, resting her head on his shoulder and rubbing his back. The two were sitting on the bed now—smack-dab between the bathroom and the door to the hall. I was trapped. "It would be hard to care about a guy I had a fake romance with in the first place!"

"I know," Dragon agreed. "At least the producers know it was fake—since they set it up. But you know they'd freak out if they knew we'd been dating for years. It would make you nominating me for this season look—well, kind of in your own interest."

Pandora nodded. "I know. And I've been trying to keep it quiet. It's sooo hard, though. Especially with you leaving tomorrow night to shoot the next season." She paused and affectionately played with his hair. "I think some of the girls in the wedding party actually think I'm after Vic, which couldn't be further from the truth."

Suddenly their conversation was interrupted by a loud *Brrring! Brrring!* Pandora jumped and turned to the phone by the bed.

"Who could *that* be?" asked Dragon.

Pandora shrugged, moving over to grab the receiver. "I told them downstairs that I broke a glass in here earlier, and I was worried about glass shards on the floor," she explained. "Maybe they're sending someone to clean it up?" She picked up the receiver. "Hello?"

The volume on the phone must have been turned up really loud, because even from my perch in the bathroom, I could hear the voice on the other end of the line. "Hello, is this Pandora Simmons?" It was Bess. She and George were trying to get me out of here!

"Yes," Pandora replied a little impatiently.

"This is room service, and we were wondering if you would like butter with the thirteen lobster dinners you ordered? Because if so, we'll need to run to the store—"

"What?" Pandora screwed up her face in confusion. "Thirteen lobster dinners? I haven't ordered anything from room service the whole time I've been here."

"Hmmm," Bess responded slowly, as though she were looking over an order. "Well, we have an order here for thirteen lobster dinners, totaling 347 dollars and 85 cents, without gratuity, of course."

Pandora was looking angry now. "Listen. I did not order those. Just cancel the order, okay?"

Bess sighed. "I'm afraid I can't do that."

"Why not?" Pandora demanded.

"You're going to have to come down to the restaurant and sign the form to void the order. I'm sorry."

Pandora let out a long, frustrated sigh. "Okay," she said, glancing apologetically at Dragon. "I'll be right down. Let's get this taken care of quickly."

She hung up the phone, shaking her head. "I'm sorry, " she said to Dragon. "I have to go take care of this, I guess. I'll just be a minute, and we can talk when I get back."

Dragon was smiling, clearly a little amused by her predicament. "All right, babe. You go tell 'em who's boss."

Pandora gave him a quick peck on the cheek, and left.

Still stuck in the bathroom, I sighed, feeling a little hopeless. Bess and George were good watchmen—they'd caught Pandora coming up, and they'd tried to give me the opportunity to get out by getting her out of the room for me. Unfortunately, they didn't know about Dragon, and he was still out there—blocking my exit.

I just hoped he didn't have to use the bathroom.

Standing up, Dragon pulled a cell phone out of his pocket and flipped it open. Looking a little bored, he dialed quickly and held the earpiece to his ear. "Hello?" he said when whoever was on the other end of the line picked up. "Hans?"

I leaned in, curious why Dragon would be calling the *Daredevils* director. "Yeah, yeah, I'm back at the hotel. I figured you were getting enough choice material without me, right?" He chuckled. "Yeah, thank goodness Vic's okay. But this wedding prank stuff is getting creepy. You sure you're not behind it?" He laughed again, more heartily this time. "No, no, I was just wondering about tomorrow. I had an idea, see. All day long, I act a little jealous of the attention Vic is getting, right? Like I'm so vain, I can't even stand this guy getting top billing on his *wedding day*." Dragon paused, apparently listening to Hans's response, and chuckled again. "I know, I know guys like that, you know? Anyway, the best part is at the reception. When the party's winding down, I challenge Vic to a fist fight!"

I leaned forward a little, peering out of my bathroom lair. This conversation was crazy! So, *was* Dragon completely faking all his actions—making up a character that would appeal to the cameras? It was hard for me to imagine, especially because I knew Syd—and surely Vic too—were almost 100 percent genuine in front of the camera crew. If Dragon started something with Vic at the wedding tomorrow, would Vic know he was faking it? Or would he be as hurt as you might expect someone whose friend is acting like a jerk to be?

Hans had apparently responded to Dragon, because Dragon was nodding his head now, looking a little disappointed. "I get it, I get it. Yeah, it might be over the top. But if nothing else happens at the ceremony, think about it, okay? You know I always bring the spice."

He laughed again. Suddenly he switched direction and started walking—I gulped. He was walking *right toward the bathroom*! *Please don't have to go, please don't have to go,* I begged under my breath. As he moved closer, I moved back, trying to fold myself behind the door, but that wouldn't hide me forever . . .

At the last second Dragon took a sharp right and opened a door close to the bathroom door. Originally

I'd assumed that was just a linen closet, but now I could hear from the street noise that it led outside— probably to a little balcony.

"Yeah, yeah, yeah," Dragon was saying. "And Pandora—she's supposed to act really upset the whole day, right? Like she's jealous or something?"

He was definitely on the balcony now. My heart leaping in my chest, I peered around the bathroom door and saw a clear path through the room to the door. Before I could think about it too hard, I darted out and ran through the room. It was only a matter of time until Pandora came back, and then I could be trapped in there for hours!

Outside the room, the hallway was empty. I was able to easily slip into a side stairway and run down to the ground floor. I came out in the hallway adjacent to the hotel restaurant, and I could hear raised voices as I slipped by on my way to the lobby.

"I'm telling you, Miss, we have no orders like that on record. We don't even *have* lobster on the menu."

"Then who called me?!"

In the lobby, soft music was playing, and Bess and George had settled on a couch in the small seating area. They both stood when they saw me approach.

"Oh, thank goodness, you got out!" cried Bess.

"Barely," I told her. "Have I got news for you! It's

notVic Pandora's hung up on—it's *Dragon*."

Bess and George's mouths both hung open. "What?" asked George. "Dragon? They're not even from the same season, are they?"

I shook my head. "No, but they've been seeing each other for years. Pandora even nominated him for the show, which has something to do with why they're keeping their relationship secret."

"So Pandora isn't the wedding saboteur?" Bess asked quietly.

I sighed and shook my head. "I don't think so," I admitted. "I *did* find a broken wine glass and scissors in her room, but that could just be a coincidence. And if she and Dragon are together, that kind of eliminates the jealousy motivation."

George suddenly looked up, behind me. "Sssshhh," she urged. "The wedding party has been trickling back in for a couple minutes. Here come Vic and Jamal."

I turned around. Sure enough, there was the blushing groom-to-be and his best man. Vic's tie hung loosely around his neck and his shirt was half-way unbuttoned. His hair stood up at crazy angles, as though he'd been raking his hand through it all night. Jamal looked a little more put-together, but they both looked tired and stressed.

"Hey, girls," Vic greeted us as they stepped closer.

"Nancy, are you feeling better? What are you girls doing here?"

"Ah . . . ," I began.

Bess rolled her eyes and threw her hands in the air in an "aren't I silly?" gesture. "I totally forgot, when we were here for brunch earlier this week, I left my shoes for the wedding in a shopping bag in the restaurant," she explained. "Nancy started feeling a little better when we got her outside in the fresh air, so I figured it was safe to swing by here."

"Good," Vic said with a nod, and I could see from his troubled expression that he wasn't all that concerned with why we were there. He looked like he had a bad case of night-before nerves, probably exacerbated by the wedding saboteur and the TV cameras. I felt a horrible drop in the pit of my stomach as it occurred to me: I *hadn't* come any closer to catching anyone. My search of Pandora's room had only brought up more questions. It looked like the wedding would go on tomorrow with the wedding saboteur still at large!

"I'm so nervous, man," Vic went on, and I could see the deep, tired lines around his eyes. "I know we'll be okay, security will be high, but I see what all these attacks do to Syd." He paused, his voice breaking. "And I can't make it better for her! It's killing me."

Jamal patted his friend on the back. "It'll be all

right, dude," he soothed. "You've been through worse before. You'll get through this."

Vic looked at his friend and blinked, tears forming at the corners of his eyes. "Thanks, man," he said, turning back to us. "Did you guys know that this guy is seriously the best friend, the best best man, a guy could ever have!"

Jamal was shaking his head. "Come on, dude. Let's get to bed."

"No, no, no," Vic insisted. "I couldn't sleep right now anyway. Do you girls have *any idea* how this guy has stuck by me? Jamal is my rock. He's been my friend through thick and thin, even after I lost him that job . . ."

"What?" The word came out of my mouth before I could think, before I could realize how impolite it sounded. And sure enough, Jamal was looking incredibly uncomfortable.

"Come on, man," he was saying. "No need to bring up ancient history."

But Vic shook his head. "Don't be modest, dude," he insisted. "These girls should know how awesome you are. Me—I can be a screwup sometimes! Which is why I'm the *luckiest guy in the world*—" Vic's voice broke again, and he paused, pulling himself together. "I'm the luckiest guy in the world to be marrying a girl like Syd." He looked at Jamal. "This guy could tell you all of my screw-uppiest moments! But he's still here. Still supporting me." He suddenly reached up and pulled Jamal into a headlock, which Jamal unhappily seemed to accept. After a quick application of noogies, he was set free.

"Jamal should have dumped me years ago," Vic went on, "when I lost him that banking job."

Jamal sighed and closed his eyes. "Seriously, dude, let's get to bed. You're exhausted and talking gibberish."

But Vic just turned to us cheerfully. "I thought it would be really fun," he went on, "to have the Knicks cheerleaders go into his office and do a cheer for his birthday—in the middle of a meeting." He laughed, shaking his head. "I knew one of them from high school, see. And I knew Jamal was a big fan. But then . . ."

Jamal was frowning, clearly not very happy about the memory. "Dude," he said, "no worries, okay?"

"His company wasn't that amused," Vic went on, his face clouding over. "Banking is pretty conservative, I guess. I should have known that. And the upshot was that I got my buddy fired." Vic swallowed, clearly holding back tears.

Jamal sighed, looking away. "It's cool, man, no big deal."

"It *was* a big deal," Vic insisted, turning to us girls

with runny eyes. "He lost his job, his salary, his stock options, everything. He'd just moved into this awesome apartment, but when he lost his job he couldn't afford the rent. He had to move back in with his parents."

Jamal just sighed, looking at the floor.

"That's when he decided to enlist in the Marines," Vic went on. "I still feel so terrible about all of that, man. I'll never forgive myself. It amazes me every day that *you* forgave me—I mean, it's not the first time I did something stupid to you!"

Jamal looked up, no trace of amusement or warmth in his eyes. "Let's get to bed," he said yet again, firmly.

Vic looked at his friend, and seemed to realize he had crossed a line. "Okay," he said, very quietly. "All right. Thanks, man. I'm sorry."

Jamal glanced at us and nodded, some pleasantness returning to his expression. "Girls," he said. "Get some sleep. See you tomorrow."

"See you tomorrow," we echoed, as the two men shuffled to the elevator and got in. The doors closed behind them, and the three of us were finally alone in the lobby.

"Did you hear that?" George asked, an expression of disbelief on her face.

"Yeah," I agreed, shaking my head. "It sounds like

Vic really did a number on Jamal's life. And Jamal seems happy in the military now, but who could blame him for holding a grudge?"

"Do you think he does?" Bess asked, looking concerned. "Do you think he could really be behind this?"

I sighed. "I don't want to," I admitted, "but it's hard not to see him as the most likely suspect right now. If he's working with Akinyi, the two of them have had opportunity, and now they have a motive." I paused. "And that would explain her terrible mood this whole time—if she thought her best friend was marrying the guy who'd ruined her flame's life."

My friends and I looked at each other, each of us clearly upset by this theory.

"But they're the best man and maid of honor," Bess said finally, voicing what each of us was probably thinking. "How could they do that to their friends?"

I yawned and rubbed my eyes. "I'm not sure they did," I admitted, "and I hope they didn't. But still—let's keep a careful eye on the two of them tomorrow."

LIGHT OF MY LIFE

"**I** think we should do a dramatic eye," Bess suggested, holding up an example from one of her fashion magazines, as all of the bridesmaids bustled around getting ready in Syd's hotel suite. "I'm thinking a smokey eye, in plum. That will really make your brown eyes pop."

"Oh, oh, I disagree," Deb Camden suddenly broke in, sweeping over to us out of nowhere. She took a look at the subject with a frown. "Did you see those pictures of Charlize Theron at the Oscars in *Us Weekly*? She did a subtle eye and a pop of color on the cheeks and lips. And she looked, you know—" She giggled. "She looked like Charlize Theron, which means *fabulous*!"

Bess turned to Deb, not looking very happy to have her expert advice questioned. "Charlize Theron has *hazel* eyes," she pointed out. "I really think a dramatic eye is the way to go."

George, who was the subject of their debate, looked over at me, her eyes pleading. I knew this was like the seventh level of purgatory for her. Before I could think of something to say to call off the makeup vultures, though, George piped up: "How about *no makeup at all,* huh? How about that?"

Bess and Deb both gasped, backing up a little as though George might be dangerous.

"You must be kidding, right?" Deb cried.

"Of course she is," Bess replied, shooting George a warning glance. "George knows that this is a *wedding,* and at a *wedding,* you wear makeup." Before anyone could protest further, she stepped in and attacked George's eyelid with a makeup brush dipped in deep plum eyeshadow. "Don't worry, George. I'll make you look like a model."

"Just what I wanted," George muttered sarcastically as Akinyi walked over, looking gorgeous in her rose-colored maid of honor gown.

"What's that?" Akinyi asked with a rare smile. "You aren't talking smack about models over here, are you?

Syd and I may look skinny, but we're fierce! We could take you on."

George smiled, or did the best she could, as Bess held down her eyelid and attacked with a black eyeliner pencil. "Of course not, Akinyi," she replied. "Hey, you're in a good mood today."

At first, Akinyi looked a little surprised by George's observation, but her surprise quickly melted away. "I am," she agreed. "Listen, I know I've been a little crabby these last few days. I guess it's just been hard for me, with the breakup, and watching my best friend go through all this scary stuff with the wedding attacks." She paused. "I guess now that the wedding is really happening and I can see the light at the end of the tunnel, I can really be happy for Syd. I mean, she's marrying the man of her dreams. This is a happy day!"

We all smiled, and I tried not to let my surprise at Akinyi's little speech show on my face. I hadn't forgotten that at the present time, Akinyi and Jamal looked like the most likely suspects to have *caused* all the strife she was talking about. But at the same time, I was hoping like crazy that she was being sincere now, and they really *weren't* behind it.

But—who else could have done it? Who else had the means and the motive?

Suddenly I became aware of the other bridesmaids

*ooh*ing and *aah*ing, and I turned to see Sydney stepping out of the small bedroom where she and her mother had been getting ready, followed by Donald and two cameramen. (Hans was part of the crew filming Vic this morning.) Syd looked unbelievably beautiful in the designer ball gown. Her long fiery hair was pinned up in a romantic chignon, and pearl jewelry shone on her ears, throat, and wrist.

"You look *so* beautiful," Bess cried, running up to hug her cousin. The cameraman focused on the two of them, trying to discreetly film the moment. "Wow! Just . . . wait till Vic sees you, coz!"

Ellie stepped out behind her daughter, misty-eyed in her pretty sage green dress, and the cameras turned on her. "I can't believe this is really happening," she said with a sheepish smile at all of us bridesmaids. "My little girl is getting married today! We actually made it!"

Syd chuckled and turned to kiss her mother's cheek. "The ceremony is going to be beautiful," she announced, "I'm sure of it. I don't know why, but I just woke up feeling really good about this day. Nothing has gone wrong so far—my dress is fine, my hair and makeup came out fine. And you know the producers have ramped up security to an *insane* degree. Maybe everything will really be okay!"

We all smiled at Syd, trying to mimic her enthusiasm, and I tried to think about what she said and whether it was really possible. It was true—security for the ceremony was going to be superhigh. Maybe she was right. Maybe, if we just let security keep an eye on the situation, the wedding really would go off without a hitch.

Of course, if the wedding saboteur really was part of the wedding party, it would be impossible to keep them out.

Donald checked his watch. "I don't mean to rush you, but it's about time to go, girls," he said.

Syd nodded. "Okay. Time to get in the limo and head to the park. Where's Pandora?"

Akinyi rolled her eyes. "Still in the bathroom, getting ready."

Without missing a beat, Syd walked swiftly over to the bathroom door, followed by a cameraman, and pounded on it with her fist. "Pandora? It's Syd. We're leaving."

Surprisingly Pandora opened the door right away. And even more surprising, she looked completely ready. "Oh, no problem," she said, taking in Syd in her dress. "Wow, you look unbelievable! I was just putting some rose oil on my pulse points." She looked at the rest of us and smiled. "Not just for the scent. Rose oil is for love—very wedding-appropriate!"

The cameras both crowded in, getting close ups

of Pandora's excited face and her rose-oil-smeared wrists. Pandora beamed angelically. I thought back to Dragon's conversation with Hans the night before. It was almost enough to make me wonder: had Pandora lingered extralong in the bathroom to guarantee this camera time? Was the "rose oil" just a cute line she had rehearsed for the cameras?

I didn't have much time to think it over, because with all of us ready (Bess had applied my makeup before George's—I had somehow gotten out of it with a "subtle eye"), we trooped out of the suite and rode the elevator down to the lobby. A few random hotel guests were clustered there in the sitting room, and they *ooh*ed and *aah*ed as we all walked by.

"Have a wonderful wedding, dear," an elderly woman advised Syd, reaching out to squeeze the bride's hand.

Syd just smiled confidently. "Oh, don't worry," she replied, "I will."

"*I* go first, *then* George!" Deb was saying as we all struggled to line up inside the Kelley Park boathouse, which was serving as our staging area for the ceremony. We were only minutes away, and tensions were running high. At least among the bridal party. I think we were really stressing out poor Donald, who'd been assigned to get us camera-ready.

"Well," he said in his quiet voice, not quite making eye contact with anyone. "Perhaps we should . . ."

"What does it *matter*?" interrupted Akinyi, who seemed to have turned irritable again the minute we hit the park. Perhaps her mood was due to the heavy security—it had taken us each half an hour to get through the metal detectors, checking and rechecking our names, and searching our purses. Most of the other bridesmaids seemed annoyed by the inconvenience, but I personally found it comforting. It was hard to imagine a scenario where any guest could sneak a weapon into the park, or anything else that could cause a calamity.

"It matters," Deb announced, "because Syd has carefully matched us up with the groomsmen. If we don't keep the right order, we could end up standing with guys that are way shorter than us! Or way taller! Is *that* what you want?"

Donald held up his hand, clearly wanting this argument to end. "Girls!" he said, his soft voice still barely audible. "If you'll just . . . if you . . . Sydney?"

Syd, who'd been staring out the window with a dreamy expression, finally turned around. "Okay, so Deb, then George," she said gently, and the bridesmaids in question fell into line. "Then Bess. Then Pandora. Then Nancy." Donald nodded gratefully as she flashed a smile at me. I took my place at the end of the line. "No offense, Nance," she assured me with a little smirk. "You know the *Daredevils* producers had to 'consult' on my procession order."

"I wasn't offended," I clarified with a smile. "This way I get to keep an eye on everybody." I was only half-kidding.

Syd nodded, turning to her best friend. "*Then* Akinyi," she said, gesturing for her friend to take her place.

But Akinyi's attention was focused out the window as up-tempo organ music began to play. *"Look!"* she cried. "The men are lining up!"

Donald seemed concerned as everyone abandoned her place to get a good look out the window. "Ladies, just . . . er . . . remember where you were!"

Deb frowned, stomping over from her place in line. "*No*, Syd!" she cried. "You're not supposed to see Vic before the wedding!"

"I think this *is* the wedding," George observed dryly.

Syd just waved her friend's concern away. "Deb, I'm just so happy to be at the part where I get to walk down the aisle," she said. "Old superstitions like that are the least of my worries." She peered out the window, smiling. "Oh, here comes Dragon!"

I couldn't help but dart a glance at Pandora, who was standing behind all of us, looking bored. She glanced up quickly, her face a little pink, and tried to catch a glimpse of her secret boyfriend. But within seconds she was back to staring at her fingernails.

"Here comes Jamal," Akinyi added, a tiny smile forming on her face as she watched the best man stroll to the altar. "And here comes Vic."

Syd moved closer to the window, pressing her nose against it as though she were trying to get closer to Vic himself. I had to admit, Vic looked incredibly handsome in his gray tuxedo with a shiny white vest and bow tie. His dark hair had been slicked into place, and he wore a huge smile that left no doubt to any of the guests as to how he felt to be marrying his bride.

"Oh, gosh," whispered Syd. "Oh, this is it. He looks amazing!"

As Syd turned away from the window, ready to take her place at the back of the line, I grabbed her hand and squeezed it. "Are you nervous?" I whispered.

Syd looked at me, seeming totally at peace. "Not at all," she replied. "I'm about to marry the love of my life. How could I be nervous about that?"

I smiled, squeezed her hand, and then let go to take my place. "Congratulations," I whispered.

Touching the earpiece he wore as though he were receiving instructions from Hans, who was set up outside, Donald nodded and reached for the boathouse door with shaking hands. "All right, ladies," he said, "when the music starts, you may start the procession."

A loud organ note sounded. But just then, it seemed like several things happened at once. There was an enormous crash from outside, followed by screams! I could hear someone yelling from the audience, "Oh my gosh! Oh my gosh!"

Then I heard someone shout, "Vic? Are you okay?"

Syd jumped out of her place in line, running to the door to get a glimpse of what happened. But Akinyi darted out first, then stepped back, restraining her friend. "It's okay," she said simply, hugging Syd, "he's okay."

Donald stepped around the two friends, looking uncomfortable as he surveyed the damage.

"What *happened*?" George demanded, her face full of concern.

Donald looked back at her, almost as though he couldn't believe it himself. "A huge can light fell down from the rafters," he replied, "but it missed Vic. Just barely."

The wedding was halted. A doctor was brought over to examine Vic, but he was quickly pronounced "okay." Miraculously, he had stepped over to ask Jamal if he had the rings just seconds before the light came crashing down. If he hadn't done that, all the wedding guests claimed, Vic would have been crushed.

It was the most dangerous stunt the wedding saboteur had tried yet.

Sydney was sitting in a puddle of white organza, sobbing, as her mother furiously tried to salvage Syd's hairdo and keep any makeup from getting on her dress. "Honey," she said soothingly. "Come on. Everyone's okay. Just keep yourself together, and we can go ahead with the wedding soon."

Sydney sniffled, looking at her mother in shock. "Mom," she cried, "my fiancé was just almost killed! I can't get married here today! What if someone gets hurt?"

I couldn't help but think she might be right. For Syd and Vic, elopement was looking like a pretty good option right now. And I couldn't help but feel like that was partly because of me—because I'd been so slow to finger a culprit. Because I'd ignored my findings last night, just hoping and praying that I'd been way off.

Off to the left of the altar, all of the major *Daredevils* players were huddled in a powwow. I knew they were debating how to proceed—go on with the wedding? Investigate what happened? Was it safe for everyone to be here?

Filled with a sudden sense of purpose, I left the

bridal party in the boathouse and walked over.

"You should report this to the police," I announced, not bothering to excuse myself or explain who I was before entering the conversation.

Fifteen sets of eyes looked up at me skeptically.

"And you are?" asked Madge Michaels, the bossy assistant director. I could tell she was looking at my bridesmaid dress and assuming I just wanted to protect my friend.

"This is Nancy Drew," Hans replied, surprising me—that he knew my name, and that he was going to show me some respect even though I'd interrupted their private meeting. "Nancy has quite a reputation in this town, I gather—she's an amateur detective."

The other crew members murmured curiously, glancing at me with surprise.

"In fact," Hans went on, "Nancy's already rid us of a traitorous bridesmaid." He smiled.

"That was *you*?" Butch, a cameraman, asked. He looked at me like he couldn't believe I could catch a mouse, much less a crook.

Of course, I was used to this.

"You should report this to the police," I repeated, turning back to Hans. "It's the most serious attack yet. Someone could have been killed. Who knows what this person will try next?"

Hans sighed. He looked at me, really seeming to

be considering my idea, but then shook his head. "Nancy," he said, "if we alert the police, we stop filming. We lose control of the situation. We lose, potentially, the thousands of dollars we've sunk into this television special." He paused. "That said," he continued finally, "we could use your help."

And he touched my arm and led me back to the "staging area," where most of the *Daredevils* crew was set up—a small square of grass across from the boathouse. A television van was parked there. Hans knocked on the door, and Donald—who'd long since left the tears and chaos of the boathouse—answered.

"I want to show Nancy the tape," Hans told Donald.

Donald looked surprised. "Are you sure?" he asked. "It's very inconclusive."

Hans nodded. "I want her to see what we're up against."

Donald retreated into the van, and Hans led me inside. The van was filled with video equipment. One television showed a black-and-white grainy image of the altar on the beach. Hans gestured to it.

"As you know, Nancy, we've been building this set for three days. The last of the lighting was put in place last night at around eleven. We left it here, guarded, and with high security—meaning cameras." He nodded at the screen. "Unfortunately for all of us, it would appear that our night watchman fell asleep last night. He's not entirely sure, but he thinks he was out from one o'clock in the morning until three. He has, by the way, been fired."

I nodded, not sure how to react. "Good?"

"Anyway," Hans said, "our saboteur would have had to have struck within that time frame. And as it happens, we did get some video footage."

He leaned over to what appeared to be a DVD player and hit Rewind. The image sprung into motion, moving backward so quickly that I could just barely make out a dark figure backing out of the frame.

Then Hans hit Play. I leaned in closer, trying to get a good look as a dark figure entered the frame from the left. He—or she—was fairly tall, but draped entirely in a huge, dark, baggy raincoat. He took a few steps, then paused and looked up—directly at the camera! I gasped. Whoever it was, the figure was wearing a black ski mask to hide his or her face. The video was so grainy I couldn't make out hair or even skin color. In one swift motion, the figure reached into a pocket and removed a can of spray paint. He or she held up the can, and the image was quickly obliterated as the wedding saboteur covered the camera lens with thick foam.

"That's it," Hans explained. "That's all we have to go on."

I was silent. Clearly that image wasn't going to lead to an arrest. Which meant that the producers had nothing. And as much as I'd pushed to report the incident to the police, I knew the River Heights Police. I wasn't entirely sure whether they'd be able to get much more than this.

"If you have any hunches, Nancy," Hans went on, "any at all, now's the time to share them. If you want to save your friend's wedding and keep all her guests safe."

I let out a deep sigh. *Jamal and Akinyi*. The names were on the tip of my tongue. They'd been around for all of the incidents so far, and one or both of them could have snuck into the park last night. And I had to admit, if I hadn't met and liked them both—and more importantly, if I hadn't known how much *Syd and Vic* loved them—I would have voiced my suspicions a long time ago.

"Akinyi and Jamal," I said in a low voice, taking no pleasure in sharing this information. "The best man and the maid of honor. Between the two of them, they were present at all the incidents, and they had the opportunity."

Hans frowned. "But why would they do it?" he asked.

"They're sort of seeing each other," I replied. "Or at least, they have in the past. And Vic lost a very lucrative job for Jamal a few years ago. Vic thinks he's forgiven him, but I don't know that he has."

Hans looked at me for a moment, as if judging whether he could trust me, and then nodded. "Donald," he said, "bring Akinyi and Jamal in here."

I felt my blood run cold. *You're going to ask them? Now?* But deep down, I knew they'd want to see how any suspects reacted to an accusation. And Hans wasn't a sleuth. If he was going to search their rooms, it would be because he got their permission and the keys to their rooms. There would be no "I lost my key" dance for the *Daredevils* director.

It probably took only a couple minutes before Akinyi and Jamal entered the van, but they felt like hours. As soon as Akinyi entered, she shot me a confused look. Jamal looked from me to Akinyi to Hans, as though he had no idea what was going on.

"Sit down," Hans urged them. They did.

"What's this about?" Jamal demanded, somewhat impatiently. "Because in case you hadn't noticed, my best friend is having kind of a rough afternoon and I'd like to be there for him."

"Me too," agreed Akinyi. "What could be so important?"

Hans looked over at me. "Nancy, would you like to explain?"

No, I thought. But I knew I had to. "Well . . ." I began, "the thing is . . ."

I broke off. How was I going to put this? The only way was just to put it all on the table.

"I've been keeping track of who was around for the different attacks on Vic and Syd . . . and the text messages that followed," I explained.

Akinyi nodded. "Okay."

I took a deep breath. "Either you or Jamal has always been present," I went on. "And one or both of you has always disappeared right as the act was taking place . . . meaning you, well, you might have done it."

Akinyi's eyes turned immediately cold. She looked at me like she'd never seen me before in her life. Jamal just sighed, putting his head in his hands with an expression like he'd been afraid this would happen.

"And *why* would I have done this?" Akinyi asked, her voice rising. "Syd is my best friend. Why would I ruin her wedding?"

I sighed. "Well, to be fair, you haven't always been very psyched to be a part of that wedding," I pointed out. "But if you're asking what your motive would be . . . I'm guessing it has something to do with Vic getting Jamal fired years ago. That completely changed your life, Jamal. I can see your being upset."

Jamal let out a short bark of laughter. "But I'm *not*," he insisted, meeting my eye. Even though I knew I was only sharing my observations, the disappointment in his eyes still shamed me. "Vic is my best friend. I forgave him, because that's what best friends do."

Perhaps sensing the tension building in the air, Hans leaned forward. "Listen," he said. "I'm sure you can understand the importance of getting this matter cleared up. Both for everyone's safety here, and for the sake of our television program. We really just want to film a wedding here, people. Not a real-life game of Clue."

Akinyi scowled. "So you think it was Colonel Mustard and Miss Scarlet in the park with the can light, is what you're saying?"

Hans shook his head. "I'm not sure of anything." He paused and looked from Akinyi to Jamal, his expression frank and curious. "Would you like to tell me where you were this morning between one a.m. and three a.m.?"

The two turned to each other, clearly uncomfortable. "Well," said Jamal. "I . . . I was in my room."

Hans nodded. "Did anyone see you? Did you talk to anyone, call or e-mail anyone?"

Jamal sighed.

"He was talking to me," Akinyi said after a moment. "I was in his room too." When I gasped, Akinyi turned to me and blushed. "We were talking about . . . us."

Hans nodded again. "But did anyone *see* you? Can anyone confirm this besides the two of you?"

Jamal frowned, clearly putting two and two together. "No," he said gravely. "It was early in the morning, after all. We only saw each other." He paused. "So what does that mean? You haul us off to jail now?"

Hans pursed his lips, as if slightly offended, and shook his head. "I would merely like your permission to look in your rooms at the hotel."

Jamal and Akinyi turned to each other, both frowning. It was clear that neither one of them were happy about this. But I knew, too, if they really had something to hide, they would hesitate.

It only took about ten seconds for the two of them to make their decision. "Fine with me," Jamal said.

"Me too," Akinyi agreed.

I traveled with Hans and a few other crew members to search Akinyi and Jamal's hotel rooms. Akinyi and Jamal followed along also, both looking grim. Whether that grimness was due to their guilt or their frustration at being wrongly accused, I couldn't tell.

"You will wait here, with these security guards," Hans told the two suspects, leaving them in the hallway under the watch of two burly bodyguards.

"Nancy, Donald, and I will look in your rooms."

Akinyi caught my eye the second before Hans opened the door to her room, and I didn't know what to say, or even what expression to put on my face. I felt terrible about all this. "Akinyi, I hope . . . Personally, I don't think you'd ever do this. The logistics just match up. Do you understand?"

Akinyi just shook her head, swiped at her eyes and turned away. Well. How could I expect her to understand?

Inside Akinyi and Jamal's room, the search went quickly. And unfortunately, it went as I'd feared.

"Does this belong to you?" Hans asked Jamal a few minutes later, holding up a dark, baggy raincoat.

"That's mine," Akinyi replied. "The baggy trench coat is all the rage in Paris right now. Why? Does it have something to do with the case?"

Hans just turned grimly to Donald, who stood behind him. Donald held up a nearly-empty can of shaving cream that we'd also found in Jamal's room. "And this?" he asked Jamal in a small voice. Does . . . this look familiar?"

Jamal sighed. "Of course!" he replied. "I used it to shave this morning. Was I supposed to show up at my best friend's wedding with a face full of stubble?"

Hans sighed deeply, turning to look at Donald and I. Neither one of us were eager to meet his eyes, but we did. "I guess," Hans said slowly, "that we have no choice."

"What, no choice?" Akinyi asked, a desperate note creeping into her voice. "What do you mean?"

Hans turned back to the couple and made a hand gesture to the guards, who grasped Jamal and Akinyi forcefully. "Akinyi and Jamal, we're going to need to turn you over to the police," Hans went on. "I'm very sorry."

SECRET BETRAYALS

"This isn't how I thought it would be," Syd said sadly, clutching her bouquet to her chest as the organ music started again.

It was perhaps two hours after Hans, Donald, and I had brought Akinyi and Jamal to the River Heights Police Station, explaining what we'd learned so far and what we thought they were responsible for. After that, we'd rushed back to the park, and Hans had gathered Syd and Vic to explain what happened. Already shaken by the events of the day, both bride and groom took the news hard, with lots of disbelief and then tears.

"I can't believe this," Vic sniffled, wiping at his eyes

with the back of his sleeve. "I trusted that guy. I love that guy! And all this time, he's hated me?"

Syd patted his back, wiping away tears of her own with a handkerchief her mother had given her. "And Akinyi," she said sadly. "She could be a little feisty, but she's my best friend. I wanted her to be here."

"Listen," Hans had said, clapping them both on their shoulders, "I know this has been a very rough day for you. But the truth is, our permits on this space run out at midnight. Now, we can give you a few minutes to pull yourselves together, go ahead with the ceremony, and film it. Otherwise, you're free to postpone—but keep in mind, the special will be ruined. And all the money you're getting will fall through the cracks." He paused, looking in both Syd's eyes, then Vic's. "Understand?"

Syd and Vic had been upset, of course, but eventually they decided that they definitely still wanted to marry each other, and that none of the crazy events of the wedding had destroyed the most important thing—their love for each other.

"Let's do this," Vic had said. "By nightfall tonight, I want to be able to call you my wife."

And so here we were, all lined up in the same row we'd been in before, minus Akinyi.

"None of you are hatching crazy plots against me, are you?" Syd half-joked as we stood in place for the second time that day. "Because I'm already down two bridesmaids. Anyone else who's against this wedding, step out of line right now."

Bess, George, and I had met eyes, then simultaneously walked back to Syd to give her a big hug.

"Sydney," Bess had said, patting her back, "you know we love you, and we're so happy for you."

Syd had given us a warm smile, dabbing at her eyes one more time. "Thanks, guys." She paused, looking behind us. "Wait a minute—where's Pandora?"

I whipped my head around. Sure enough, our flakiest bridesmaid was missing again—no big surprise there. Sighing, I told Syd I would find her. She was probably just outside the boathouse "meditating" again. Really, it seemed a little far-fetched now that we'd ever considered such a space cadet capable of the crimes Akinyi and Jamal had committed.

I opened the back door to the boathouse, the one that opened away from all the guests and commotion, and sure enough, I heard Pandora's distinctive voice.

"Yeah," she was saying with a mean chuckle, "it's kind of hard to be happy for him after the jerk broke off our million-dollar TV series because he was soooo in love with Syd. I mean, I get it, but can't you just play for the cameras? Like they always want us to do? Like we did all season? Hold on . . ."

I was frozen in place. *Million-dollar TV series? Play*

for the cameras? What was she talking about?

It took me a minute to realize that Pandora had placed her hand over the phone and turned to face me, smiling her usual spacey smile. "Are they ready, Nancy?"

"Yes," I said simply. "We need you inside."

"No prob." Pandora smiled again and picked up her phone. "I'll call you back later, sis. Got to go be a bridesmaid."

She flipped the phone shut, stood up, and followed me back inside.

My mind was racing a hundred miles an hour, but I had no time to do anything. The music was already playing. The groomsmen were getting into place . . .

"Deb!" I cried suddenly, grabbing Deb's arm as Pandora ran over to give Syd a last-minute hug. "Do you know anything about a TV series with Pandora and Vic? Something he might have turned down?"

Deb's eyes grew wide and she nodded. "Oh, sure," she replied, the corners of her mouth turning up. "Pandora and Vic were such a popular couple on the show, the producers wanted to follow them around for a year while they dated—sort of a *Newlyweds* type thing, except they hoped without the breakup at the end!"

I nodded quickly. "But Vic said no?" I asked.

Deb nodded. "He did. Because right after their

season of *Daredevils* wrapped, Vic met Syd and fell head over heels in love with her!" She giggled. "Isn't that romantic! He turned down five hundred thousand dollars to star in that show with Pandora. But he listened to his heart."

She paused, no doubt taking in my stunned, glassy-eyed expression. "Are you okay?"

"Places!" Donald cried, suddenly springing up out of nowhere to open the boathouse door. "Nancy! I need you in place!"

Out of the corner of my eye, I was vaguely aware of Bess and George shooting me confused looks as I walked back to my place in line—behind Pandora, in front of Syd.

He turned down $500,000. Meaning that he'd kept her from getting that amount of money, too. Meaning that Pandora *did* have a reason to get revenge on Vic—even if they never had been a real couple.

Pandora turned and smiled at me. I'm not sure whether it was intentional, but it chilled my blood. I gripped my bouquet tight as Vivaldi's "Spring" started playing and Bess began walking down the aisle.

No time to ask questions now, I told myself as Pandora began walking, then me. We exited the boathouse, and 150 guests turned eagerly to watch us.

Cameras flashed, the bright sunlight got in my eyes, and I could see Vic beaming as he watched us—and then his bride—walk down the aisle.

I just have to keep a close eye on her.

12

A DANGEROUS MAID

"**W**e are gathered here today," the minister intoned, as we all settled into our places at the altar, "to join Victor Josiah Valdez and Sydney June Marvin in holy matrimony."

As Vic and Syd beamed at each other, I turned my full attention back to Pandora. Her annoyance at Vic that she'd been voicing on her phone just a few minutes ago seemed to have dissipated, and now she watched the happy couple with a huge smile. But was it real? Or was she just playing for the cameras? Playing to the TV audience seemed like something both Pandora and Dragon were very good at.

"The importance of joining two lives together in

marriage cannot be overstated . . . it is the cornerstone of our society, and . . ."

As the minister droned on, I let my attention shift to the audience, still watching Pandora out of the corner of my eye. After all the drama and danger of getting the ceremony moving, it was almost easy to miss how truly beautiful the *Daredevils* producers had made the park. Huge bouquets of pink peonies studded the aisle and each side of the audience. And the altar was positively overflowing with flowers! At the end of the aisle, and on either side of the altar, the cameramen tried to be as unobtrusive as possible— but still captured all the action.

In the audience, I saw several people dabbing at their eyes. I understood how they felt. After all the action of the past few weeks, it felt amazing to know that in a matter of minutes, Vic and Syd would be man and wife.

As long as I could keep Pandora from trying anything!

The minister was introducing the vows Syd and Vic had written for each other.

After they exchanged vows, the minister called over George's brother, Sebastian, who was now serving as best man, to produce the rings, and he quickly led Vic and Syd through the ring exchange. I was so busy fighting tears, so happy for my two friends who were about to start their life together, that I almost forgot what was coming next. But no sooner did the minister say . . .

"If anyone here knows any just reason why these two should not be united in marriage, let them speak now or forever hold their peace."

. . . than I turned my full attention to Pandora. And I was stunned by what I saw!

She'd been so peaceful through the ceremony up till that point, but as I watched her in amazement, she reached into her bouquet and pulled something out—something long, silver, and sharp-looking.

". . . I now pronounce you man and wife!"

It was a knife! And she was moving now—headed toward Syd and Vic!

"Nnnooooooooo!" I screeched, lunging from my place at the altar and tackling Pandora—rose taffeta dresses and all!

As you might imagine, total chaos broke out as I struggled to pin Pandora to the ground.

"Nancy!" she was screaming. "What are you doing?! What's gotten into you?!"

But within seconds, a trio of security guards were surrounding us.

"What's the problem here, Nancy?" one of them asked me. I looked up and recognized him as Jeff—one of the guys who had accompanied us to the hotel to search Akinyi and Jamal's rooms.

"She has a knife," I said quickly, backing up to let the security guards handle Pandora. "In her bouquet. She had pulled it out and was advancing on Syd and Vic!" I paused, trying to take in a breath. "I think we may have been wrong about Jamal and Akinyi."

Pandora looked from me to the security guards to the stunned audience, clearly upset. "It *was* a knife," she admitted, "a ceremonial knife! I wasn't going to *hurt* Syd and Vic—I was just going to perform a traditional wedding blessing."

Hans had emerged from behind the cameras, and he looked doubtfully at Pandora—and the large, sharp knife she had fished out of her bouquet. "I don't know of very many rituals that require advancing on a married couple with a knife," he said drily. "Pandora, we're going to want to search your room."

Suddenly Pandora burst into tears. "Fine!" she cried. "I know I'm innocent!"

As Hans prepared to head to the hotel with a couple security guards, and other guards moved in to take control of Pandora, I glanced over at Vic and Syd. They had retreated from the action and were quietly hugging each other at the other end of the altar. Vic stroked Syd's face as they both glanced over at Pandora, then she leaned up to kiss him.

They're married now, I thought happily.

And no one—not the wedding saboteur or anyone—could take that away from them.

"You're not going to be happy," Hans warned Pandora as we all waited for him to tell us what he and the guards had found in her hotel room. It was perhaps forty-five minutes later, and the entire wedding party, along with Syd, Vic, and their close family members, had settled in the boathouse to wait to learn Pandora's fate. Pandora, who was still restrained by two burly men, just looked at Hans and wiped away a tear.

"I don't see how that's possible," she insisted, "since I'm innocent."

I glanced at Dragon. It must be hard for him to see his secret girlfriend accused in this way! Unless . . . had he been in on it? I remembered the conversation I'd heard where he'd offered to be cruel to Vic on his wedding day, to spice things up. Of course, he hadn't needed to.

Things had turned out plenty spicy on their own.

Hans took a breath, then blurted, "We found a broken glass and a pair of scissors in your hotel room."

Pandora scoffed. "Okay—so what? I dropped the glass when I stubbed my toe a couple nights ago. Maid service still hasn't picked it up. And the scissors are for my collage art."

"Collage art?" asked Vic, looking skeptical.

Pandora glared at him. "I'm a very creative person," she insisted. "I need an *outlet*!"

Hans nodded. "Well, that's all fine and good. But the truth is, those two things aren't nearly as disturbing as our other discoveries."

Pandora's face fell. "Which are?"

Hans motioned to one of the guards, who handed him a huge, baggy raincoat. "This," he replied, as the guard reached into a bag and then pulled out some shaving cream, "and this. Clearly you used these when you broke into the park and disabled our light."

Pandora looked stunned. "But—but—those aren't mine!" she cried. "I've never seen those things before in my life."

"Haven't you?" Hans asked, warily. "How about this?" And he reached into his pocket and pulled out a stack of printed papers with handwritten notes in the margins. I leaned in for a closer look: the handwriting was loopy and girly, just like I would imagine Pandora's to be.

Pandora squinted at them. "I don't think so," she said. "What are they?"

"A detailed guide to common lighting setups for television and movie shoots," Hans said, waving them in the air. "Printed off the Internet. And with notes in the margins like, 'cut the two side cables, but leave the electrical cord hanging' . . . I suppose you're going to tell me you just have a *strong creative interest* in lighting?"

Pandora looked utterly shocked and confused— as though she'd never heard of the Internet at all. Slowly, though, her face changed. She reached up to wipe her eyes, and my heart sank at the sight of her expression—she looked completely, utterly defeated.

"They're not mine," she said quietly. "That's similar to my handwriting, but it's not mine."

"Then how did they get there?" Hans demanded. "What were they doing in your room?"

Pandora just sobbed.

"And what about your motive?" Donald suddenly piped up. He'd traveled to the hotel with Hans, again, and was standing a few feet behind him. "Vic dumped you and turned down that television show that would feature the both of you. He broke your heart and lost you a lot of money, didn't he?"

Pandora looked down at the floor and blinked. "Yes," she said quietly.

"And that made you very angry, didn't it?" Hans broke in. "In fact, I remember you had a few choice words for me when I gave you the news."

Pandora looked up at him, tears shining in her eyes. "I was upset," she agreed, "but I didn't do this."

Subtly—probably barely noticeable to anyone who

wasn't looking for it—Pandora turned to Dragon. She gave him a meaningful look, but what did it mean to convey? *You know I didn't do this? You set me up?* What?

I waited—it felt like minutes, but was probably only a few seconds—for Dragon to speak up. To explain to the world that Pandora and Vic had never really been together—that she loved *him,* and always had. Dragon looked haunted, like he was witnessing something horrifying, but he remained silent.

After a few seconds, he looked away.

"We have to take you to the police, Pandora," Hans said, moving closer to her.

Pandora sobbed. After a couple of seconds, she wiped her eyes and seemed to try to get a hold of herself. She looked around at everybody, her eyes stopping when she reached a stone-faced Syd and Vic, who had remained surprisingly quiet and uninvolved throughout this whole process. I thought they were just trying to focus on the fact that they were married now—whatever the wedding saboteur had taken from them, they would soon be starting their new life together.

"I'm sorry," whispered Pandora. "Syd and Vic, I'm so sorry this happened to your wedding. I swear I didn't do it."

Vic watched her for a moment, then swallowed.

"I'm sorry," he said in a breathy voice, "but I don't believe you."

Guards advanced on Pandora, and soon she was being led out of the boathouse, into a waiting car that would drive them to the RHPD. I assumed—or hoped, maybe—that once Pandora was in custody, Akinyi and Jamal, who it seemed were innocent after all, would be set free.

I watched Dragon as his secret girlfriend was led away. He watched her, looking sympathetic, until she reached the door. Then he turned away, glanced around the room, and disappeared into the men's room.

I wished I knew what he was thinking.

"Well," Hans announced, once Pandora had been removed from the boathouse. "This has been a long, exhausting day, but we still have some celebrating to do! Syd and Vic, do you want to go ahead with the reception?"

Syd and Vic looked at each other. "Are you sure?" Syd asked, honest concern clouding her face. "I know this must be especially hard on you, Vic. To know someone you used to love would do this to us . . ."

Vic bit his lip. Looking extremely uncomfortable, he turned to Hans, who sighed and finally nodded almost imperceptibly. "Tell her," Hans agreed. "She has the right to know now. And it won't change anything."

Syd looked confused. "Tell me what?" she demanded. "Vic, don't tell me you've been keeping a secret about the case."

Vic shook his head. "Of course not, no," he insisted. "I would never keep anything from you that might lead to your getting hurt. But the truth is . . . Pandora and I . . ." He paused and sighed.

Syd watched him carefully, looking like the suspense was killing her. "What?" she cried.

Vic smiled. "We were never really a couple."

Totally confused, Syd looked from Vic to Hans and back to Vic. "Huh?" she said.

Hans nodded, stepping closer. "They were never really a couple," he confirmed. "Vic's season of *Daredevils* was coming out a little lackluster, so . . ."

Syd frowned. "So?" she repeated.

"So we asked Pandora and Vic to spice it up," Hans explained.

Syd looked back to Vic, stunned, as Vic took her hands and said soothingly, "Pandora was *never* my type, babe. Nothing mattered more to her than being on camera. I would have told you a long time ago, but . . ." He trailed off, gesturing at Hans and Donald.

"But?" Syd prompted.

Donald cleared his throat, turning a little red. "It

would have broken the confidentiality agreement that all players sign," he explained.

Hans nodded. "Of course, with everything we've had to worry about these last few days, your breaking that agreement is the least of our troubles."

Syd stared at Vic thoughtfully, then shook her head. "I can't believe it!" she said with a sheepish chuckle. "All this time I was fighting my jealousy of Pandora. All the experiences you had together, the feelings she might still have for you . . ."

Vic smiled. "All fake," he confirmed. "Ever since I met you, Syd, you're the only girl that matters. So shall we go celebrate?"

Syd laughed and nodded, and Vic turned to Hans.

"I'm so happy to be married to this girl, I need to *dance*!"

Vic's pronouncement cut the tension in the room like a knife slicing through butter. Soon everyone was laughing, talking, speaking eagerly of the reception and the lavish party that awaited us.

Vic took Syd's hand and led the way out the door. "Let's get this party started!"

"Oooh, look," Bess whispered, looking up from her fizzy pink punch as a couple new figures entered the party: Akinyi and Jamal.

"So they *were* set free," I observed, feeling a strange

combination of guilt and relief. After all—I was more responsible than anyone for getting them sent to the police station in the first place. And it now appeared that they were completely, 100 percent innocent.

"Nance," George said gently, squeezing my shoulder. "Don't beat yourself up. You had plenty of reasons to believe what you did. And you just wanted to keep everyone safe."

I watched Akinyi and Jamal, not ready to reply. The reception had been going on for a couple of hours, and Syd and Vic were whirling dreamily on the dance floor. Everyone else was dancing or mingling cheerfully over punch and wedding cake. Cameramen swooped in and out, trying to capture, but not control, the action.

"I have to go apologize to them," I announced, looking at my friends with a guilty expression. "Sure, I had reasons to believe what I did, but I must have embarrassed them completely—plus I kept them from witnessing their best friends' wedding. I feel terrible."

Bess looked sympathetic and nodded. "So let's go apologize," she suggested. "George and I will come with you."

We made our way across the dance floor. As we approached, Akinyi turned and saw me and sighed deeply. She didn't look angry—but she did look disappointed and exhausted. I could see that talking to me was not high on her "to do" list.

"Akinyi, Jamal," I said quickly and loudly, before I could lose my nerve. "I just want to say I'm very sorry. I was trying to use logic to solve the case when I accused you, but I know all the evidence was circumstantial—and, as it turned out, totally wrong." I sighed. "I'm so sorry. You're both such good friends to Syd and Vic, and I helped ruin their wedding for you."

Akinyi looked away, like she didn't want to deal with this, but Jamal looked at me and nodded. He didn't look thrilled, but he did seem to be impressed by my apology. "I understand how you got to your conclusion, Nancy," he said simply. "It may take us a while to get over this, but we don't blame you, okay? We just want to enjoy the reception as much as we can and tell our friends how happy we are for them."

I nodded. All in all, the two of them were being very gracious. "I'll leave you to it, then," I offered, but just as I spoke, Syd came barreling out of nowhere and tackled Akinyi in a hug.

"Akinyi!" she cried, followed closely by her new husband, Vic. "I'm so sorry. I know nothing I say will ever make this right. And I'll never forgive myself for doubting you, or for keeping you from being part of my wedding."

Akinyi, who had looked stiff and uncomfortable since entering the reception, seemed to soften a little. "Syd," she said, her voice rough, "just don't do that again, okay? You know I love you."

Syd pulled back and looked her friend in the eye. "I do," she said sincerely. "I really do, Akinyi. And I'm so sorry it took something like this for me to realize it."

Meanwhile Vic held out his hand to Jamal. "It looks like I owe you for a lot of things, buddy," he said, his own voice sounding pretty close to tears. "I'm so sorry. I should have known you would never hold a grudge."

Jamal nodded, looking very serious, then a smile peeked out. "I know you're a jerk, Vic," he said, starting to chuckle. "It's part of what I love about you, okay? You're larger than life."

Grabbing Vic's hand like he was going to shake it, Jamal pulled his friend close and they embraced.

"I'll never forgive myself," Vic said, sounding sincere.

"I know," Jamal said simply, "but I will. You be good to this woman, and have a long happy marriage, and we'll call it square."

Syd smiled, gesturing to me. "If it weren't for Nancy, we never would have figured out it was really Pandora causing all the trouble," she told Jamal and

Akinyi. "Thank goodness she's so observant! Without her, we'd be headed off to the Caribbean still feeling afraid." She turned to me. "Nancy," she said, "I know this hasn't been an easy case for you. You've had to make a lot of tough decisions, and hurt a lot of feelings." She paused. "How can Vic and I ever repay you?"

I smiled. "It's just like Jamal said," I replied. "Have a long, happy life together, and forget all of this ever happened."

Vic turned to his bride with a big smile, squeezing her hand. "Done, and done," he promised me.

UNEXPECTED CONTACT

"**O**kay, I thought Syd and Vic's wedding was nonstop action," George told Bess and me a few days later as we piled into my kitchen after seeing a movie. "But that was the most action I've *ever* seen crammed into two hours."

"Definitely," I agreed. "When they blew up that trailer?"

"Or when that lion showed up?" Bess added, shaking her head. "He was *hungry*."

I sighed, happily settling down at our kitchen table. It felt so nice not to have to worry about dresses, or shoes, or fittings, or cameras, or threatening messages. Syd and Vic had left for their honeymoon on a remote Caribbean island the day before, and their silence seemed to indicate they were having a perfectly normal honeymoon.

"What's going on with Pandora?" George asked, finding some chocolate chip cookies in the cookie jar, freshly baked by our housekeeper and unofficial caretaker, Hannah.

"She's still being held by the police," I replied. I'd called the RHPD for an update just that morning. "They're testing some of the evidence they found in her room for fingerprints, DNA, that sort of thing. She still insists those printouts, the raincoat, and the shaving cream were not hers."

Bess shuddered. "She seemed so harmless and spacey all week," she commented. "Scary to know how dangerous she really was."

"Nancy?" I looked up and spotted Hannah standing in the kitchen doorway, pulling the vacuum cleaner behind her. "Did you see you have mail? It's on the counter."

I sprung up. "Anything important?" I asked. "Or is it something boring, like my cell phone bill?"

Hannah smiled. "It's postmarked from London," she replied. "And it was sent express mail. Who do you know in London?"

I glanced at Bess and George, honestly confused. "I have no idea," I replied.

Getting up and walking over to the counter, I found a thick, business-size envelope addressed to "NANCY DREW" in messy, all-caps handwriting. Sure enough, the return address was a Thistle Kensington Gardens hotel in London. Curious, I tore open the envelope and pulled out a thick stack of paper with a sticky note on top:

> Here are some things you should know. The wrong person is in jail. The crook is still out there! you have to do something. Sincerely,
>   A concerned citizen

"Whoa," I breathed, as Bess and George got up to peer over my shoulder.

"Wasn't *Daredevils* starting out its season in London?" Bess asked.

"I think you're right," George confirmed. "So Dragon would be there—and most of the crew we worked with."

Peeling off the sticky note, I turned my attention to the papers beneath. The first seemed to be a photocopied page of a contract—upon further inspection, it seemed to be the contract *Daredevils* contestants signed that outlined the rules and regulations they must follow to compete in the show.

One section in particular had been highlighted in orange marker:

"No contestant shall have any current or prior connection to anyone involved in the production of *Daredevils*. This includes producers, crew members, employees of the FUN television network . . ." I paused, breathing in. ". . . or prior contestants." I gave a meaningful look to my friends, who seemed to get it immediately.

"Dragon and Pandora," Bess whispered.

I nodded, reading on. "If producers or crew members become aware of any such association during the filming of *Daredevils*, the contestants involved will be ejected from the show, and any monies paid to the contestant, either in the form of winnings or appearance fees, will be returned to the production company."

George whistled. "So if Dragon and Pandora made their relationship public, they'd both lose a bunch of money. Whatever they received for appearing on the show, plus any money Pandora won."

Bess nodded. "And Dragon would be kicked off this season," she added. "Which is kind of a big deal, since he's favored to win."

I flipped through the papers, turning to the next page, and gasped. It was a printout of a typed page titled "Traditional Wedding Blessing." Scanning the paragraph, I picked up on bits and pieces: "The officiant then waves the knife over the couple's heads, chanting ... the knife must be very sharp, symbolizing the threats the couple will face to their union ..."

At the top of the page was a handwritten note:

Pandora—would make a great scene if you could perform this on the couple after the ceremony!

My jaw dropped. The handwriting was identical to the handwritten notes in the margins of the printout the producers had found in her room!

I heard Bess breathe in sharply behind me. "You know what this means, don't you?" Bess asked.

I nodded, slowly putting the papers back down on the counter. "Pandora was set up," I replied. "And Dragon wants us to know about it."

Just then a musical *beep* sounded from my purse on the table. I glanced at my friends. It had to be my phone—and the tone of the *beep* told me it was an e-mail.

I walked over to the table, pulled out my phone, and sucked in a breath as I flipped it open.

YOU HAVE 1 NEW E-MAIL FROM SYDNEY VALDEZ.

I pushed the buttons to open it.

SOS. NANCY, I NEED THE THREE OF YOU HERE NOW!
IT'S NOT OVER!

·   ·   ·

There were four attachments, which I opened one by one. The first three were e-tickets—one each for George, Bess, and I to join Syd and Vic on their semiprivate island.

The final attachment was a photo. It showed what must have once been a beautiful hotel room—now totally trashed. Wrecked furniture—so battered and broken, it looked like it had been bashed into the walls—was piled around an unmade bed, with torn bedding strewn everywhere. On the bottom sheet, scrawled in a red liquid that looked like blood, was a chilling message:

Enjoy being newlyweds. You won't both be alive for long!

On the bottom of the message there was a messy red smear. I pointed, my stomach clenching nervously. "What *is* that?" I whispered to my friends.

George blinked, shaking her head as it came to her. "It's a silhouette," she breathed. "For Mr. Silhouette."

Gulping, I leaned in. I could see it now: the dark profile, eyes, nose, mouth. "Syd's stalker." I shivered.

"Oh my gosh," whispered Bess. "I guess we're

headed for the Caribbean! Because Mr. Silhouette is still on the prowl."

George stared at the photo, nodding grimly. "And he's upped his game," she pointed out. "From saboteur—to *murderer*."

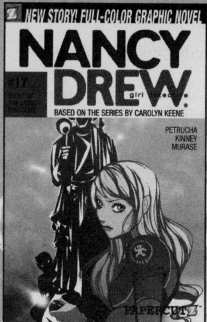

Tell your BFFs to meet you on Beacon Street!

Join the Tower Club at **BeaconStreetGirls.com** for Super-cool virtual sleepovers and parties! Personalize your locker and get $5.00 to spend on Club BSG gifts with this secret code

To get your $5 in MARTY☆MONEY (one per person) go to www.BeaconStreetGirls.com/redeem and follow the instructions, while supplies last.